CRESCENT CITY WOLF PACK

6

# SHIFTING FATE

CARRIE PULKINEN

This is a work of fiction. Names, characters, places, and incidents are either the product of the author's imagination or are used fictitiously, and any resemblance to actual persons living or dead, business establishments, events, or locales, is entirely coincidental.

Shifting Fate

COPYRIGHT © 2021 by Carrie Pulkinen

All rights reserved. No part of this book may be used or reproduced in any manner whatsoever without written permission of the author except in the case of brief quotations embodied in critical articles or reviews.

Contact Information: www.CarriePulkinen.com

Edited by Krista Venero

ISBN: 978-1-957253-04-6

# PROLOGUE

France, early 1600s

Alrick's heart raced as he approached the cathedral. His feet ached from the long journey, but it would soon be worth the pain. A full moon illuminated the stone architecture, the gargoyles perched atop the towers casting soft shadows in its light. A massive circular window was situated in the center of the structure, and three pointed archways held entrances to the chapel.

As instructed, Alrick passed by the doorways and made his way down the left side of the church to a small wooden door near the back. He pulled a folded piece of parchment from his pocket and hesitated to perform the secret knock.

Once he passed through this threshold, there would be no turning back.

But he owed it to his country and his people. Vile creatures had been allowed to run rampant in the villages for long enough. Magic was an abomination, and it needed to be wiped from the face of the earth. The forsaken must be destroyed.

With a deep inhale, he rapped the rhythm on the wood. The door swung open to reveal a long, dark corridor. Torchlight flickered some twenty meters ahead, and as he stepped through the entrance, the door slammed shut behind him. The hall made a sharp left turn where the torch burned, and he followed it to a set of stone steps leading down beneath the main floor.

Excitement hummed in his veins as he descended the staircase. The Sect recruited only the most skilled warriors for its new supernatural army, and Alrick was among the first to receive an invitation. He accepted without hesitation, for how could he refuse being part of the dawn of a new age? An age without magic smearing the face of humanity.

Marie's words echoed in his mind as he reached the bottom of the stairs, and he paused again. "You don't have to do this, Alrick," she'd said. "If you love me, you can find it in yourself to love all beings, mundane and magical alike."

He was indeed in love with Marie, but he loved the woman, not the witch. His feelings for her had bloomed before he had learned about her magic, and he had continued to care for her in spite of her abominable powers. If there were a way to strip the magic from her soul, he would have done so. Alas, leaving her was his only option. To do otherwise would be duplicitous.

Pushing thoughts of the witch from his mind, he continued toward a foreboding set of arched double doors. He knocked the secret rhythm on the wood once more, and the sound of a lock disengaging echoed through the corridor. A man in a deep red robe opened one of the doors and motioned for Alrick to enter.

Five men, warriors from neighboring villages, stood in a line in front of a raised dais. Seven Sect leaders, all in red robes, save for the Supreme, who wore black, sat in ornately carved wooden chairs atop the platform. As Alrick joined the men, the Supreme rose and lifted his hands. Alrick and the others dropped to one knee, bowing their heads in reverence.

"It is with great pride that I, the Supreme Leader of the Sect, initiate the first order of the gargoyle warriors. Your sacrifice for the greater good will forever be remembered and honored. Please rise and remove your doublets and jerkins."

Alrick did as requested, stripping until he stood before the Supreme in only his breeches and boots.

"Magic is a plague on this land, and you, my brothers, will end its reign. Behold." The Supreme descended from the dais and strode toward a great red crystal, at least two meters in diameter, sitting on a stone platform.

"This is Thropynite, the stone that will enable a demon to fuse with your soul. Once the fusion takes place, you will be granted shapeshifting abilities and become the greatest warriors known to man. Under the cover of night, you will transform into your demon and raid the villages, killing everyone suspected of practicing magic. Witches, sorcerers, werewolves, and the like will cower at your feet, but you will show them no mercy, for..."

"The Sect is the one true creed, the Supreme our only leader," they all said in unison.

"As you are aware, your sacrifice is great. When the earth has been rid of magic, you, as magical beings, will be destroyed. Is this sacrifice done willingly?"

"Yes, Supreme." Adrenaline coursed through Alrick's veins. The ultimate sacrifice for the ultimate act of faith.

"Proceed." The Supreme nodded to a Sect member who wore thick leather gloves and a mask. The man used a chisel to break off five pieces of the red stone. With each hit of the hammer, a thunderous boom echoed in the chamber and sparks ignited, illuminating the dimly lit room as if lightning had struck.

"Who shall be the first to accept his initiation?"

Without hesitation, Alrick stepped forward. "I will, Supreme."

The Supreme inclined his chin. "Very well."

Two men took Alrick by the arms and escorted him to a circle carved into the stone floor. A five-pointed star occupied the diameter, and they positioned him in the center of the shape before forcing him to his knees. Alrick obeyed willingly, for he was about to become the first gargoyle warrior for the Sect, an honor he not only deserved, but one he would treasure for the rest of his existence.

The Supreme drew his hood onto his head and read from a leather-bound book. He spoke Latin, a language the warriors did not understand, but as the atmosphere in the room thickened, the intent behind his words was clear.

Holding a dagger horizontally in both hands, the Supreme chanted and then kissed the blade. He handed it to a Sect member, who entered the circle and pressed the tip to Alrick's sternum. Alrick clenched his jaw as the blade pierced his skin. A burning sensation spread through his chest, and the Sect member dragged the tip downward, opening his flesh.

Alrick held in his groan. He had sustained far worse injuries on the battlefield, yet the pain from this small incision ricocheted through his body, making him want to scream in agony. He gritted his teeth, for a true warrior never showed weakness.

The Sect member placed the shard of Thropynite into the wound, and the pain intensified threefold. A traitorous moan escaped Alrick's lips, and the Sect member squeezed his shoulder.

"It will be over soon, my friend."

The Supreme resumed his chant, filling the room again with the energy of lightning. Blood dripped down the center of Alrick's chest, the stone sizzling inside the lesion. A low vibration filled the air, increasing in volume until all he heard was the hum throbbing in his ears.

Alrick's heart raced, and as he peered at his torso, the trail of blood reversed direction, flowing upward and returning to his wound. The circle and star ignited, a wall of fire surrounding him, licking upward to the ceiling. His blood ran cold as the heat, hot as the fires of hell itself, consumed him.

He squeezed his eyes shut, willing his body to bear the pain of being burned alive, when a guttural roar filled his ears. He opened his eyes to find a demonic spirit floating in front of him. Black smoke swirled, taking the shape of a gargoyle, its grotesque mouth, much too big for its face, curling upward into a menacing smile.

Alrick's body tensed in fear. He wanted to run, for even a celebrated warrior like himself was no match for a creature without a physical body. But he was frozen to the spot. The demon snarled, and Alrick swallowed the sensation of a lump of burning coal from his throat.

The Supreme's chanting rose above the noise, and the demon shot toward Alrick, the impact knocking him onto his back. He lay prone, unable to move as the fiend invaded his body, battling with his psyche.

Alrick felt hands on his arms, though his vision had tunneled to mere pinpricks of light. The sensation of being dragged registered in his mind. His arm was lifted, his hand placed against a smooth stone. Another flash of agonizing pain. His chest tightened, the wound healing instantly, the shard of stone embedding in his skin.

As the demon fused with his soul, his hatred of the forsaken grew tenfold. Burning anger seethed in his veins, and he rose, bowing his head to the one true leader. "On my life and my honor, I vow not to stop until every last trace of magic has been vanquished from this earth."

The Supreme bowed in return. "Take your place by my side, brother, as we initiate the others. Your faith has earned you the title of general in our army."

The gargoyle warriors began their crusade that very night. Alrick could never have dreamed the satisfaction he'd feel as he tore the forsaken limb from limb. The taste of their blood on his tongue. The sensation of their bones snapping beneath his fingers. The pleasure almost masked the ache in his heart for the one he'd left behind.

# CHAPTER ONE

With the magic of the full moon humming in his veins, Noah L'Eveque paused on the corner of Royal and St. Philip, across the street from O'Malley's Pub. Tilting his head toward the sky, he inhaled deeply, closing his eyes and focusing on the low vibration in his muscles, the faintest hint of the nearly imperceptible shifter magic flowing through his soul.

Sticky summer air clung to his skin, and as a bead of sweat rolled down his forehead, he flicked it away with a finger. He could almost feel the blast of chilly air that would greet him in the doorway of O'Malley's as he stepped inside, and the draw of his pack's headquarters had his legs moving toward the building involuntarily.

He stopped on the edge of the sidewalk and peered through the window at the activity inside. While the shifters of the pack followed the call of their wolves to the forest to hunt, the rest of them—Noah included—felt little more than an extra burst of energy in their magic this time of the month. A dozen people—all second-borns or non-shifting mates—gathered around the bar, talking and imbibing the free drinks offered monthly, every full moon.

Who said shifters had all the fun?

Normally, Noah would have been inside with them, enjoying the comradery of his fellow second-born weres. He hadn't missed a full moon gathering in as long as he could remember, but tonight, he couldn't bring himself to step inside.

And it was no mystery why.

Amber, the alpha's sister, stood behind the bar, laughing with the others, her blue eyes sparkling with her smile. She'd swept her light golden-brown hair into a ponytail, revealing the delicate curve of her neck, and as she glanced at her watch and bit her bottom lip, an ache expanded in Noah's chest.

Her shift would be ending soon, and if he went in now, she'd join him at the bar, stay there with him 'til closing time, long after the others called it a night, and make him feel things he shouldn't for a woman in the alpha line.

His feelings had intensified so much over the past few months, he could hardly look at her without the crushing need to sweep her into his arms and make her his. But Amber deserved better. She'd made that clear. With alpha blood flowing through her veins, she should be with a shifting wolf.

*Fuck.* His hands curled into fists. Noah should have been a shifting wolf, goddammit, and if fate hadn't played games with his future, Amber would be his mate by now.

Only first-born werewolves gained the ability to shift… around the age of thirteen…except in a case like Noah's. His older sister was his twin, and if they'd been born closer together, they both would have become shifters. But Noah was breech, and the umbilical cord was wrapped around his neck, complicating his birth. He didn't make his appearance into the world until half an hour later…too late for his magic to activate his wolf gene, leaving him no better than any other second-born werewolf.

Gritting his teeth, he strode past the entrance and made a left on Bourbon Street, heading into the heart of the French Quarter. He needed to get the woman off his mind, and with his friends out hunting, the excitement of New Orleans' most famous street was the next best distraction.

He wiped the scowl from his face, straightening his spine as he strolled into the throng of people and pushing the what-ifs from his mind. *It is what it is.* Focusing on what was, rather than wallowing in what should have been, had served him well enough. Being angry at fate didn't do anyone any good. Besides…things might be changing for him soon.

Laughter and chatter drifted on the air, and the brassy sounds of a jazz band blasted from the open door of a club on the corner. He stopped at the to-go window and bought a beer. Chilled air seeped out from the inside, taming the Louisiana heat as the bartender filled a plastic cup with frothy goodness. Noah took a long sip, savoring the cool, bubbly liquid as it slid down his throat, and he continued on his way

There was no better place than Bourbon Street for people-watching. College-age partiers all the way up through the occasional couple in their seventies came here to forget their worries and indulge in a bit of sin before heading back to the monotony of real life. The energy of the city called to people, enticing them to tear down their walls and let the good times roll.

"*Laissez le bons temps rouler.*" Noah chugged his beer and tossed the cup in a trash can before stepping inside a club. A cover band blasted an early 2000s pop hit from a small stage near the entrance, and three women in their forties laughed as they danced, trying to entice their husbands to join them on the floor.

Noah made his way toward the bar, but he stopped short when a brunette backed against a wall caught his eye. She gripped her beer bottle, her nails digging into the label as her gaze darted about the room, looking at anything but the hulking man who had her cornered. She swallowed hard, and a nervous giggle bubbled from her throat. The asshole took it as an invitation, reaching toward her and running his fingers down her cheek.

Without a second thought, Noah moved toward them. If he were a shifter, his mere presence would be enough to intimidate the man into backing off, but he wasn't. He'd have to get creative.

"Hey, sis, sorry I'm late." He held out his arms in an invitation for a hug.

The woman furrowed her brow at first, but as the asshole crossed his arms and puffed out his chest, she recognized Noah's attempt and stepped into his embrace. "I thought you'd never get here."

She hugged him quickly and stayed by his side, forcing a smile. "What took you so long?"

"Got hung up on the jobsite." He wrapped an arm around her shoulders. "Who's your friend?"

The man grunted, took a swig of his beer, and, as he stomped away, Noah couldn't help himself. He called on his magic, gathering the energy into his hand until he could feel the atoms in the atmosphere. With a flick of his fingers, he nudged the man's foot with his power, causing it to catch on his other ankle and making him stumble.

The man caught himself, inflating his chest and looking around as if to be sure no one was laughing at him. Noah held in a chuckle. Served the bastard right. He should've sent him flat on his face.

All second-born weres possessed a psychic ability. Some were empaths, while others could talk to the dead or get glimpses of the future. Noah's telekinesis was a power many envied, but he would give it up in a heartbeat to awaken his inner wolf. Maybe someday…

As the man disappeared into the crowd, the woman's breath came out in a rush. "Thank you for that."

Noah released her shoulder. "You looked like you needed a little help. Are you here alone?"

"My friend is in the restroom." She held out her hand to shake, and a flirtatious smile curved her lips. "I'm Tiffany."

He accepted. "Noah." Her skin was warm, but no magical energy sparked from it. Like ninety percent of the people in New Orleans, she was pure human. Her wavy hair brushed her shoulders, and as he released her hand, she tucked one side behind her ear.

"Jeez, Tiff. I leave for five minutes, and you've already picked up a guy. I hope he has a friend," a blonde with dark brown eyes said as she approached them.

Tiffany laughed and clinked the neck of her beer bottle against her friend's. "This is Noah. He saved me from a drunk. Noah, this is Caitlyn."

"Hey." She nodded at him and turned to Tiffany. "This place is lame. Let's get out of here."

"Okay." Tiffany tossed her bottle in the trash and tilted her head at Noah. "Do you want to come with us?"

"Do you have a friend?" Caitlyn batted her lashes.

"It's just me tonight, I'm afraid."

Tiffany bit her bottom lip and swept her gaze down his body. This could be just the distraction he needed.

"Hmm…" Caitlyn shrugged. "I suppose we can share. Come on." She linked her arm through his and tugged him toward the door. Tiffany clutched his other bicep and followed.

Noah instinctively glanced over his shoulder and found the drunk from earlier glaring at them as they made their way toward the exit. With a flick of his hand behind his back, Noah knocked the bottom of the guy's glass, spilling his drink down the front of his shirt.

*It's not parlor magic.* His buddy James's words echoed in his mind. *It's a unique werewolf gift.*

Not the gift Noah was meant to have…

But he made do with the magic he was given.

He chuckled as they exited the club and turned toward the next one, but his chest tightened, giving him pause. He had an attractive woman on each arm, and a few months ago, he would have been *so* down for this. Now, he couldn't stop imagining Amber's disappointed expression as she chewed her lip and glanced at her watch earlier this evening.

He was supposed to be there with her. He was *always* there for her. What the hell was his problem now?

He tugged his arms from the women's grasp. "It was nice meeting you ladies, but I think I'm going to call it a night."

"But it's early…" Tiffany said, disappointment evident in her eyes.

"I have somewhere to be. Y'all stay safe tonight. Stay together." He nodded and strode to the other side of the street before they could argue more.

Tugging his phone from his pocket, he glanced at the time and cursed under his breath. He needed to march his sorry ass back to O'Malley's and spend the evening with Amber like he had every full moon since gods-knew-when. He should wad up his emotions, shove them into the darkest corner of his mind, and be the best friend he was supposed to be. That was all she wanted from him.

He, Amber, and his twin sister, Nylah, had been inseparable since they were kids. Nylah going rogue shouldn't have changed things between Amber and him. He'd always had feelings for her, from the time he was old enough to understand what feelings were.

They weren't reciprocated, and he understood why. A telekinetic second-born had no place in the alpha line. Amber should mate with a dominant shifter, someone who would pass on the genes a true leader needed.

He'd hinted at his feelings for her once, and she'd shut him down quickly. "I'm so glad we're friends," she'd said. "It's nice not having to worry that you're after me for my pack status." That was when things had gotten awkward, and he'd needed to put an end to that. He could never be the werewolf she needed, but he could be her friend.

"Where is she?" A woman's frantic voice drew his attention down the street. "Goddammit, Mitch, where did she go?"

The woman, in her fifties or sixties, with platinum hair and a thick coating of blue eyeshadow, clutched a bouncer's shoulder outside a strip club and gave him a shake. "You're supposed to take care of my girls."

Mitch shrugged off her grasp and stalked to the end of

the building, peering at the closed gate blocking the alley before marching back. "A guy dropped his wallet. I stepped inside for half a minute to return it, and when I came out, she was gone." He shook his head. "I'm sorry, Angel. She probably got a good offer from a tourist."

Angel shook her finger in his face. "My girls are *not* prostitutes. They're dancers."

Shoving his hands in his pockets, Noah shuffled toward the gate and nudged it with his shoulder. It swung freely, so he slipped inside the alley, freezing as the coppery scent of fresh blood assaulted his senses. Though his night vision wasn't nearly as sharp as a shifter's, there was no mistaking the heap of flesh lying crumpled at the end of the passageway.

Pulse thrumming, he moved toward it, his gaze darting about the darkened corridor, searching for the culprit. Muffled music from Bourbon Street filtered in through the gate, masking any sounds of retreat, and a trash can overflowing with three-day-old garbage made it impossible for him to catch a scent. He focused his magic into his skin, feeling the hum of the atmosphere around him. No living energy interrupted the flow. Whoever did this was long gone.

He crept toward the body, covering his mouth as he took in the gory scene. The woman lay on her back, her right leg bent at an unnatural angle. Blood soaked her once-blue satin bra, and in her chest, a jagged, gaping hole was all that remained where her heart used to be.

His stomach turned, and his hand trembled as he dialed the alpha's mate and pressed the phone to his ear.

"Detective Mason speaking."

He swallowed the lump from his throat. "Macey, it's Noah. I found a body in the Quarter. It looks supernatural." He described the scene and the events leading up to it.

"Have you contacted Luke?"

"I will. I don't think her boss has even called the police yet. The killer is long gone, so I thought you should know."

"Who's on patrol with you? Cade or James?"

He hesitated to tell her the real reason he hadn't called the alpha first. "I'm...alone."

She missed a beat in her response. "You're patrolling by yourself?" The wariness in her voice was a knife to his heart. Non-shifters weren't allowed to patrol alone. Macey was the only exception, and that was because she'd been a detective for longer than she'd known she was a second-born werewolf.

"I was at a bar across the street, saw the commotion, and came to check it out." The last thing he needed was to get into trouble with the alpha. His position on the hunting team was fragile as it was.

"Okay." Relief was evident in her voice.

"Don't worry. You don't have to report me."

She paused, the sound of a car door slamming through the receiver filling the silence. "It's not a law I agree with, if that makes you feel any better."

"Thanks. What do you want me to do?" He looked around for any signs of the culprit but found nothing. Whatever took this woman's heart had to have massive claws or a wicked weapon.

"Get out of the alley and call Luke. If you can't reach him, follow the chain. I'll take care of the humans."

"Hey!" Angel's voice echoed down the alley. "What are you doing?"

"Shit." He flicked his wrist, swinging the gate toward

her and knocking her back into the street. He cringed at the sound of flesh hitting pavement and scrambled to climb the fence.

"Get back here, fucker!" Mitch plowed through the gate as Noah's foot slipped.

He fell to the ground, smacking his head on the cobblestone, and his vision swam. Mitch hauled him up, slamming him against the brick wall.

"What did you do to her, you sick bastard?" Mitch pressed his forearm into Noah's chest, squeezing the breath from his lungs.

*Shit. What now?* He glanced around the alley, searching for something he could grab with his mind to fight back, but Angel's agonizing wail pulled his attention to the body.

"Bridget!" She dropped to her knees, folding forward at the waist and covering her face. "Oh my God, someone call the police."

Half a dozen dancers hesitated at the alley entrance before creeping forward, their faces pale, expressions distorted in shock as sirens blared in the distance.

Noah was toast. He stopped struggling, and Mitch eased off his chest enough for him to speak. "I didn't touch her. The alley gate was open, so I came in to look for her."

Mitch's eyes narrowed into slits. "Save it for the police."

Another bouncer, even meatier than Mitch, if that were possible, sidestepped around the dancers and grabbed Noah's arm. He could have fought back, but his second-born strength was no match for these beefcakes. Noah would have to use his magic to have any chance of winning, and he couldn't do that in front of all these people.

Instead, he let them drag him to the street and cooperated as the police put him in handcuffs. Tiffany and Caitlyn, the women he'd met at the bar, stood on the sidewalk a few feet away, but he couldn't meet their eyes.

He had royally fucked up. Whatever the human cops had planned for him would pale in comparison to the punishment waiting for him once he returned to the pack. *This* was the reason non-shifters weren't allowed to patrol alone. They lacked the speed and strength to get out of situations like this. A shifter never would have been caught.

As the officer guided him into the back of the squad car, he caught a glimpse of Macey's face before she headed into the alley. The disappointment and pity in her eyes was enough to tear him in two.

A werewolf arrested by the human police. He was a disgrace to his pack.

## CHAPTER TWO

Amber Mason strolled next to her mother up St. Philip Street toward O'Malley's Pub. The hot June sun beat down on them, heating the top of her head and making her reconsider the bar's standard black uniform. It was too damn hot for dark colors.

The surprise lunch visit had been pleasant, her mom filling her in on her parents' move to Jackson, Mississippi, and how her dad was settling into his new role in the werewolf national congress. They talked about family and how Amber was handling running the bar on her own, Debbie placing just enough emphasis on the *on her own* part to make it clear this visit wasn't simply social.

But Amber wasn't taking the bait. If her mom had something to say about her current relationship status—or lack thereof—she'd have to work it into the conversation on her own. Amber sure as hell wasn't bringing it up.

"How long are you in town for?" She opened the door and gestured for her mom to go inside.

Debbie paused and looked at her, tilting her head and giving her that *I can't believe you haven't found a man* look.

It was unmistakable: the way her brows drew together and lifted at the same time, the twitch as the corners of her mouth tried to pull into a frown but she forced them upward into an awkward smile.

It was the look of pity, and though Amber favored her mom, with the same light-brown hair and blue eyes, she tried her best to avoid the facial expressions that somehow cut deeper than words.

Her mom placed a hand on her shoulder, giving it a gentle squeeze before she stepped through the door. "Just for the afternoon. I'm heading to Lake Charles to visit Vanessa this evening and staying a few nights there."

Chilled air blasted Amber's skin as she crossed the threshold, a welcome relief from the sauna of the Louisiana summer. Shaded lights hung from exposed beams in the ceiling, giving the quiet bar a dark, smoky haze. A couple sat in the corner, sharing an order of loaded fries and a pitcher of beer, and Chase stood behind the bar, chopping a lemon.

He lifted his head and grinned as he caught sight of Debbie. "Afternoon, Mrs. Mason. Where's the old man? You leave him behind this time?" He stood on a plastic crate and leaned over the bar, stretching out his arms in invitation.

Debbie smiled and leaned in to hug him across the bar. "Us girls need to have a little fun without our mates every now and then. How are you and your witch?"

Chase chuckled and rubbed a hand down his dark beard. "We're good. Perfect, in fact."

"I'm so glad you found someone." She gave Amber the side-eye and leaned against a barstool, crossing her arms over her pressed white blouse.

Amber fought her eye roll. "I'd offer you a drink,

Mom, but since you're driving, we better not. I'll tell Luke you said hi."

"Actually…"

*Oh lord. Here it comes.* She'd all but dismissed the woman. Couldn't she go on her way without bringing up the inevitable?

"I was hoping we could talk somewhere privately about a family matter."

Apparently, she couldn't. Amber rolled the stiffness from her neck. The headache this conversation would bring was already inching its way into the base of her skull.

She gestured to the side door. "We can go in Luke's office. There's more room in there." And it wasn't in the same state of perpetual disarray as her own office. She didn't need to give her mom anything else to chide her for.

Debbie strode toward the door. "Is your brother here? That would be even better."

*I wish.* Luke would make the perfect buffer for this conversation. He'd been through all this with their parents already. "He's on a jobsite."

"Too bad."

Amber followed her mom through the swinging door, down a short flight of brick steps, and into the back corridor. A storage room filled with cases of beer and restaurant supplies opened up on the right, and she reached across to the left, pulling her office door shut as she passed it.

The alpha's office lay just beyond the storage room, and Debbie didn't stop to knock before she pushed the door open and disappeared inside. Amber stood in the entrance as her mom ran a hand across the back of a green chair, a sad smile playing on her lips as she stepped toward the massive oak desk and picked up a small Eiffel Tower figurine on the corner.

"I remember when this was your father's office."

"Yeah, well, it wasn't that long ago." She dropped into a chair and crossed her legs. "What did you want to talk about?"

That same scrunched-brow look of pity contorted Debbie's features. "You're twenty-nine years old, sweetheart."

She folded her hands in her lap. "Last time I checked."

A small chuckle emanated from her mom's throat. "You get your sarcasm from your father."

"And his alpha blood and all the laws that come with it. Is that what you wanted to talk about?"

Debbie laced her fingers together and leaned against the desk. "You're obligated to take a mate by the time you turn thirty."

"Which is ridiculous."

She held up her hands. "It's not my place to agree or disagree with the law, but it is *the law*. I don't want you to go through what your brother did if you wait until the last minute."

"You mean when he found his fate-bound, but *the law* almost forced him to mate with someone else when they ran into trouble? Don't worry, Mom. That'll never happen." Amber wasn't meant to be anyone's fated mate. If a wolf in the pack was going to claim her, it would have happened by now. "No one wants me."

"That's not true. Any man in the pack…in any pack… would be happy to take you as his mate. You have—"

"Alpha blood. I know." And that was the perfect reason to spend the rest of her life with someone, wasn't it? Not because he loved her, but because she could bring him into the inner circle, give him a child with alpha blood. *No, thank you.*

"It's within your brother's authority to select someone for you."

Amber's mouth dropped open. Was her mother actually suggesting she let Luke *assign* someone the task of mating with her?

Debbie slid into the chair next to her and patted her knee. "He would never choose your mate, dear, but if there's someone you had in mind, he could…" She shrugged.

"Do you hear yourself, Mother? If I were a man, would you suggest I force a woman to become my mate? Take away her choice, her free will?" Her parents were so old school it was a wonder she and Luke turned out the way they did. This wasn't her father's pack anymore, and she would not succumb to these crusty old antiquated laws.

"No, that would be different."

"It's exactly the same."

Her mother pursed her lips and blew out an irritated breath through her nose. "Your brother nearly brought shame upon our family…in front of the congress, no less. If things hadn't worked out for him the way they did, the congress could have brought in new leadership. Our family could have been exiled."

Her heart sank. Luke *had* to have a mate to become alpha. While Amber would never hold any position of authority, it was her obligation to ensure the bloodline continued undiluted.

"Your father could lose his place on the congress if you… Please don't put our family in another situation like that."

"I won't. I've got plenty of time to find someone I can stomach spending the rest of my life with."

Her mom frowned. "You have six months."

Amber's smile faded, and she placed her hand on Debbie's. Where had the time gone? "I won't let you down."

Her mom rested her free hand on top of hers. "You never have. If there aren't any men in the pack who pique your interest, we could plan a soiree. Plenty of men from the neighboring packs would love to meet you."

"No. Absolutely not. This isn't the 1800s." She tugged her hand from her mother's grasp and stood, pacing around the desk. No way in hell would she allow herself to be put on display like that. She was a grown woman, for Christ's sake.

Debbie nodded. "You're right. That would make you look desperate."

"Which I'm not." She'd dated a couple of pack members when she was in her early twenties. It had quickly become obvious they were more interested in her position than her personality when they preferred having dinner with her parents over spending time alone with her.

"No, you're not." That damned look of pity crossed her mother's face again before she smoothed her features and rose to her feet. "I had better hit the road. I've got an early dinner reservation." She glided toward the door, pausing and turning to Amber. "I almost forgot to ask. How's Noah? You didn't mention him at lunch."

A flutter formed in her stomach, but it quickly turned sour. "I haven't heard from him in nearly a month."

"That's odd. He's one of your best friends."

*Was* one of her best friends. When he skipped the full

moon gathering last month, she'd assumed he was on patrol with Cade or James. But when he didn't respond to her texts the next few days, she'd received the message loud and clear.

"I think he must have met someone." Saying it out loud, the words solidified into steel and pierced her heart. Noah was never serious about anything, especially dating. Whoever was occupying his time these days must have had her hooks in him deep.

Her mother's pity face twisted the blade. "I'm sure he would have told you if that were the case. Noah's kindness and concern for others are some of his best qualities. Wonderful qualities for a potential mate." She raised a brow.

If she was trying to plant a seed in Amber's mind, she was wasting her time. The idea that her feelings for Noah ran deeper than friendship had sprouted a while ago, but right before she could express her interest in him, something about their relationship had changed. He'd backed off, acting awkward around her. She didn't dare risk ruining their friendship by trying again. He was the only single man in the pack who didn't look at her as a breeding machine.

Amber crossed her arms. "I'm sure he'll make a great mate for *someone* someday."

Debbie's lips curved into a sly smile. "I'm sure he will. Give your brother a hug for me. I'm sorry I missed him." She blew a kiss to Amber and slipped into the hall.

Gritting her teeth, Amber shuffled to the door, waiting until her mom exited into the bar before making her way to her own office. She dropped into a high-backed leather chair, spinning in a circle as she chewed her bottom lip. As the chair came back around to face the desk, she planted her feet on the floor and let her elbows thunk on the wooden surface.

She inhaled a deep breath and let it out slowly, willing the tension in her shoulders to ease. That conversation could have been worse. At least this time her mother didn't suggest she lay off the fatty bar food if she ever wanted to land a man. Still, the insinuation that Amber's greatest contribution to the pack would be having a baby sat sour in her stomach like expired buttermilk.

Her second-born psychic ability was occasionally useful. So what if she only had gut feelings about the future and could rarely give specifics? She'd given the pack a heads up about danger on several occasions. Who knew what would have happened if she hadn't? And she ran this bar and maintained the offices and innerworkings of the pack headquarters. This place would fall apart without her, dammit. She didn't have time to fuss with a man.

Unless that man was Noah.

Fisting her hands, she pressed her knuckles against her brow, squeezing her eyes shut and willing the thoughts away. But her will didn't work on her feelings for her friend any more than it did on easing the tension creeping toward her temples.

Her mother was right about one thing: Noah did have all the qualities of a good mate. He was kind, honest, funny, smart, and... Lately she'd begun to find him physically attractive as well, which was weird. Growing up, even when the other girls in school were fawning over him, she'd never thought of him in that way.

Something had changed in the past year, though, and now she couldn't look at the man without a smile tugging at her lips and warmth blooming in her belly. He had thick, auburn hair she wanted to run her fingers through and dark brown eyes she could imagine sparkling with mischief in the bedroom. A shiver shimmied up her spine.

Maybe it was hormones…what shifters called their mating instinct. Amber's wolf was dormant, but it was possible she still had the reflexes. She was getting dangerously close to thirty, and while the arbitrary deadline placed on her was fabricated by the ancient geezers in the congress, most werewolves did find their mates around this age.

After watching her brother find so much happiness with his fate-bound, Amber decided she would never mate with a shifter unless his wolf claimed her as his own fate-bound. She couldn't take that opportunity away from any man. It wouldn't be fair.

Noah's wolf was dormant too, so it didn't matter that he hadn't claimed her. He wouldn't be claiming anyone. Not as a fate-bound…but perhaps as a soulmate just the same. Even humans believed in that concept, so why not?

Whatever it was, she couldn't deny she had feelings for her best friend. She also couldn't deny the jealousy burning in her chest at the thought of him spending so much time with another woman. He could've at least had the decency to reply to Amber's text and let her know he'd be indisposed for the rest of his life.

Especially after what happened with Nylah. Amber and Noah had both been crushed when his twin went rogue, abandoning them without so much as a goodbye.

It seemed hasty departures ran in the family.

She snatched the pile of papers strewn across her desk and shuffled them into a neat stack, tapping the edge against the wood to even them out. It was time to get her life in order. She had an obligation to the pack, and pining over a man who was obviously not interested in her would only hold her back.

The office phone rang with an internal call, and she hit the speaker button. "Yes?"

"Shipment just came in," Chase said. "If you'll man the bar, I'll move the cases to storage."

"On my way." She ended the call and rose to her feet, stretching her arms above her head before rolling her neck and straightening her spine. Her mother was gone, so she could forget all about the ordeal…until her next visit.

She strode through the hallway into the bar, where Chase had stacked four cases of Abita onto a dolly, and the front door swung open before Luke stepped through. She took two strides toward her brother, but Noah entered the bar behind him. Her heart slammed against her chest, and she froze. He hadn't spoken to her in nearly a month, and *now* he showed up at her bar? *Oh, hell no.*

"You can stay here, Chase. I'll move this to the back." With her foot on the crossbar, she pulled the dolly toward her, angling it onto its wheels.

"You sure?" Chase asked. "It's heavy."

"I've got it." She glanced at Noah, and his eyes brightened. Before she could get sucked into their depths, she trained her gaze on the floor and hurried through the door to the storage room.

## CHAPTER THREE

Noah's chest tightened the moment he looked into Amber's crystal blue eyes, all the feelings he had for her—which he'd tried to wad up and shove deep down inside him over the past month—bubbling to the surface and making his heart ache.

He didn't realize how much he'd missed her until now, and when she turned on her heel, hurrying to the back without even acknowledging him, all the effort he'd made to squelch his emotions dissolved like a sugar cube in a cup of hot coffee. *Ouch.*

"Great to have you back, man." Chase nodded from behind the bar, and Noah glimpsed a new tattoo near his collarbone. The letters R and A in a cursive script disappeared behind his shirt, most likely his mate's name: Rain. What else had Noah missed in his absence?

He followed Luke through a side door and down the brick-lined hallway into the alpha's office. His stomach soured as he sank into the green vinyl chair. The last time he set foot in the pack headquarters, he was put on a three-week-long probation—a light sentence for his transgression. He was essentially under house arrest, not allowed to communicate with anyone in the pack, aside from his immediate family, and only allowed to leave his home for work. Even then, he'd had to stay by Luke's side like a puppy on a leash at the jobsites.

Noah worked for Luke's construction company, so lucky him, he got to be babysat by the alpha himself. To say it was humiliating was an understatement.

The police still hadn't found the killer, not that they would. The murder had supernatural written all over it. It was a good thing both the alpha's mate and her brother-in-law were on the human police force. They were able to pull some strings and get Noah released with no charges filed.

Now, he'd served his punishment for breaking pack law, and he could have his life back. Lesson learned.

Luke sat in a black office chair behind the desk, and it squeaked as it absorbed his weight. He opened his laptop, punching a few keys before peering at Noah over the screen. "Your probation is officially lifted. Thanks for complying. You made my job a little easier."

"Yeah, of course." What else could he do but comply? If he'd gotten a wild hair and tried to leave his house, he'd have been thrown in the pit—the werewolf prison. Stephen, the alpha's cousin, spent three months in the pit before his exile, and he nearly went insane from the isolation. Noah shuddered to think about it. "I swear I won't patrol alone anymore. That was a stupid decision."

The alpha grunted. "I shouldn't let you patrol at all. The congress would have my head if they knew a non-shifter had taken on watch duties."

Noah's heart sank. He'd worked his ass off proving he was worthy of his spot on the demon-hunting team. "I'll be careful. I won't hunt without a shifter, and if I'm out alone and see something, I'll call it in."

Luke pressed his lips into a thin line, narrowing his eyes before he nodded. "Screw the congress. Times are changing, and your ability is like no other. There's been another murder. We need all the help we can get." He closed his laptop. "Welcome back."

A flush of relief loosened the tension in his chest, his shoulders relaxing as the weight of yet another possible humiliation lifted. "Thank you. I won't let you down again."

The alpha stood and gestured to the door, so Noah bowed his head and strode into the hallway. Luke followed him toward the bar, but as they passed the storage room, Noah paused. Amber stood on the third rung of a ladder, sliding a case of beer onto a shelf.

"Hey, Luke," she said. "Mom came by and said to tell you 'hi.'"

He chuckled. "How did that go?"

She gave him the stink eye. "Same as before. It would've been nice if you'd been there to help me out."

"Maybe next time." He winked and strode into the bar, but Noah hesitated in the doorway. Amber stepped off the ladder and picked up another case.

"Let me help you with that." Noah sauntered into the room and gripped the box. As his hand brushed hers, her magic vibrated across his skin, sending a jolt straight to his heart. All supernatural beings had a magical signature, and Amber's felt so warm and inviting, he couldn't help but imagine his hands gliding across her bare skin.

She jerked the case away and climbed the ladder. "I don't need help." She shoved the box onto the shelf and turned to pick up the next one, but Noah already had it in his hands.

"I've got nothing better to do." He smiled, which earned him a scowl. "Is everything okay?" He set the box on the shelf, using his power to slide it into place.

Amber huffed and stepped off the ladder. "Oh, so we're pretending like nothing happened?"

"*Did* something happen?" He'd been on probation for three weeks, so whatever it was, he'd missed it.

"Seriously?" she scoffed. "You stood me up on the last full moon and then ghosted me. You think you can come back nearly a month later and act like it never happened? What? Did your new girlfriend dump you?"

"Whoa. Amber, that's not what happened. I didn't ghost you for a woman." He stepped toward her, gently gripping her arm.

Her breath caught as she cast her gaze to where he touched her, but she didn't pull away. "Where were you then?" Her stiff posture relaxed slightly, and she angled her body to face him.

"I ran into trouble patrolling alone, and I got arrested on my way to the bar that night. I've been on probation ever since." He cocked his head. "Wait. You haven't heard from me in three weeks, and you didn't ask anyone what might have happened?"

Her mouth opened and closed before she swallowed hard. "I didn't want to know."

*Wow. Okay.* He gave her arm a squeeze and released his grip. "I could have been dead."

"Then we would've had a funeral." She shook her head. "I assumed you met someone and were done with me. After Nylah left without saying a word, and then you… I was hurt." She lowered her gaze.

"Hey." He hooked a finger under her chin, lifting her head. "I would never abandon you. Okay?"

"Okay." She looked into his eyes, and something sparked in her gaze.

He couldn't recall her ever looking at him like this before, and it was all he could do to stop himself from leaning in and taking her mouth with his. Judging from the way her body drifted toward him, she might have let him do it.

He cleared his throat, breaking the trance he'd succumbed to. "You really had no idea what happened to me?"

She blinked, stepping back as if trying to shake off the electricity that had just charged between them. "If it was something bad, I would have known. That's kinda my thing."

"True." Amber's gut feelings weren't always about the future. Sometimes, she just *knew* things.

"And with all the summer festivals going on, there have been too many tourists in the bar for the guys to talk openly. Luke and Chase have been hush-hush about pack dealings lately, so I never heard them mention you."

*Yet you still didn't bother to ask…* That hurt more than he cared to admit.

"I'm sorry to put you through that. Whenever I do meet someone, you'll be the first to know." He winked, attempting to lighten the mood, but the thought of being with anyone but Amber sat heavy in his stomach like his grandmother's meatloaf.

She flashed a tight-lipped smile. "Good to know. I…" Her gaze blanked, and she swayed slightly for a moment before she cocked her head at him. "Have you heard from Nylah at all?"

"Not since the day before she left." He clamped his mouth shut. That was a lie. His sister did leave without saying goodbye in person, but he'd found a note on his nightstand the morning she went rogue. Nylah had written that she couldn't tell him where she was going or why, but she promised to return with an answer to his prayers.

The only prayer he'd had was to activate his dormant wolf gene…something Nylah was determined to make happen. Since then, he'd received several cryptic texts from untraceable numbers that could only have been his sister. *I think I know how to find it; it won't be long now,* and *got it* were just a few of the messages she'd sent.

"I have a weird feeling about her." Amber pulled the band from her hair, slipping it onto her wrist before scratching her head. "I think she might be in trouble. No…she's about to be in trouble."

His pulse raced. "Details? Is she close?"

"I don't…" She squeezed her eyes shut, her face pinching as if she were trying to force the empathic magic to expand. "Maybe?"

"Both of you. In my office." Luke stood in the doorway and jerked his thumb toward the hall, making Noah tense. The alpha did not sound happy.

---

Amber followed Noah and Luke into the office and sank into a chair. She felt like an idiot for assuming Noah had met someone and tormenting herself for weeks. If she'd asked her brother about him when he didn't reply to her texts, she could have saved herself a world of hurt. That was what she got for acting fickle, and from this point forward, she would behave like the strong, independent woman she was. And she'd start by telling Noah how she felt.

As soon as she worked up the courage.

"Tell me what you're feeling about Nylah." Luke leaned on the edge of his desk. "Do you have any details at all?"

"Not yet. The feeling is still building." She closed her eyes, focusing on the impending doom wriggling in her mind, but it was no use. Her ability never could be forced, and the more she tried to will the feeling to expand, the more mixed signals she'd receive.

Luke nodded, cutting his gaze between her and Noah. "I'm going to let you two in on a secret, but this information is not to leave this room. Understood?"

"Yeah, of course," Noah said, and Amber nodded.

"Nylah didn't go rogue. She's working for the congress."

Amber blinked, and Noah let out a long, slow breath. "Come again?" she said.

"The congress approached all the alphas, asking each pack to nominate a shifter to go undercover. She's been traveling the globe, gleaning magical information and helping stop mayhem before it begins."

She looked at Noah. "Did you know about this?"

He shook his head. "She never said a word."

"She wasn't allowed to." Luke strode around his desk and sank into his chair. "She was instructed to leave in the middle of the night without telling anyone, making it appear like she went rogue. Until now, I was the only person who knew."

A mix of emotions swirled through her chest, taking her from happy to relieved to anxious, all in a matter of seconds. Her lips tugged upward before pulling down into a frown, and her brow furrowed, lifting and lowering. She didn't know what she felt at the moment, but she was positive her old friend was about to find herself in a heap of trouble.

"Do you know where she is?" she asked. "Someone needs to warn her."

"I don't," Luke said. "She isn't allowed to communicate with anyone from the pack, including me."

When Noah shifted in his seat, Luke squared his gaze on him. "You two were always close. Have you been in contact with her?"

"I'm in just as much shock as Amber. I have no idea where she is."

"I'll put a call in to the congress. Amber, if you get any more details, let me know." He dismissed them, and Amber followed Noah into the hallway.

"Do you really not know anything?" she whispered.

A strange look gathered in his eyes like sadness mixed with uncertainty. "She abandoned us both."

"Apparently, she didn't. I don't know what to feel about this news, but I'm glad to know she left without saying goodbye for a reason."

Noah raked a hand through his hair, his mouth opening and closing as if he wanted to say something.

Before he could utter a word, sharp pain flashed in Amber's chest, the sensation like claws dragging down into her stomach. This was not good. *So* not good. She blinked up at Noah. "Whatever's going on with her, it's about to go downhill fast."

## CHAPTER FOUR

Alrick crouched on the sidewalk next to a shop entrance and ground his teeth as he observed the people in their strange clothing walking about, drinking colorful liquid from peculiar vessels, shouting, and laughing in a most obscene way. He'd never witnessed such debauchery in his entire existence.

He'd also never witnessed so many magical beings residing in one location. His demon side longed to destroy them all. It was what he was built for, but he was still too weak to perform his duties.

Duties he'd shirked for a traitorous witch…

It had been almost a month since he'd last ventured out. The heart he'd consumed then wasn't nearly enough sustenance, and he'd needed time to mend and adjust to life. Consuming another heart would help replenish his strength, but he required the Thropynite stone to restore all his powers. A piece of it was close. He could feel it in his bones.

He closed his eyes, opening his senses as he rubbed the tiny sliver embedded in his chest. The Thropynite—a magical crystal from his homeland of Europe—was the source of his power, the only thing that kept him from turning to stone, but the shard he was gifted long ago wasn't enough to give him life. Another piece had found its way to this continent…to this very city now…awakening him from his slumber.

He would find it.

As he opened his eyes, he took in blue trousers and strange red shoes. Lifting his gaze, he discovered a man smiling at him.

"Nice gargoyle costume, dude. Can I get a picture?"

Alrick growled, swiping a hand at the insolent male. He didn't venture out of his pocket dimension for revelry. He was here for sustenance and information.

The man lifted his fists, bouncing on his toes as he laughed. "Uh-oh, someone wants to fight."

Alrick's lip curled. He didn't sense magic running through the imbecile's veins, but the man reeked of alcohol and cigarettes. That was reason enough to eliminate his existence.

Alrick's bones creaked as he rose to his full six-and-a-half-foot height. It was time he gained the knowledge of the years he'd lost.

"Wow. That costume really is amazing." The man took a step back, but Alrick clutched his shirt.

"What century is this?" His voice grated against his throat like gravel, coming out as more of a croak than words.

"Dude, what's your problem?" The man grabbed his hand, trying to pry his talon-like fingers apart, but even in his weakened state, Alrick's demon soul gave him the strength of fifty men.

"I asked you a question," he rasped before clutching

the man by the shoulders and dragging him into the alley next to the building. As he slammed him against the wall, the man's head knocked on the brick before lolling to the side.

"What century is this?" He gripped the sides of the human's face, straightening him, and his eyes fluttered before opening into slits.

"It's the 2000s, man," he muttered.

Alrick grunted. It had been nearly three hundred years since his duplicitous witch left him, taking the Thropynite with her and forcing Alrick and his brothers into slumber. "You will show me all you know."

He tightened his grip, digging his claws into the man's scalp, puncturing first skin and then bone. As the life force oozed from the man's head, Alrick absorbed his memories.

Four decades of life flashed through his mind, the human's knowledge of history filling in the gaps and bringing Alrick up to speed with the current times. How things had changed during his slumber... It was all he could do to not go berserk on these fools and murder them all. They had no inclination of the devilish magic that moved among them.

Releasing his grip from the man's head, Alrick plunged his claws into his chest, ripping out his barely beating heart. As he consumed the organ, his spine straightened, the cracks in his stone-like skin beginning to mend before splitting again, causing him to hunch over in pain.

It was time he returned to his pocket dimension to process the new information he received and formulate his plan to find the stone that had awakened him upon its arrival to this land.

In a flash of magic, he transported himself to the woods on the outskirts of the city, the place he and his brothers had been banished to long ago for their grotesque appearance. He sighed as he gazed at the shimmering film over the entrance to his home and then let out a dry chuckle. It was more of a prison than a home.

As he lifted his hand to swipe aside the magic, he felt it. His back straightened again, and his frigid blood hummed in his veins. The stone was closer than it had ever been before.

A growl rumbled from behind him, and he spun around to find a copper-colored wolf snarling at him. Her muzzle peeled back, revealing sharp fangs, and her intelligent eyes sparkled with magic. This was no normal wolf.

She lunged, latching on to his shoulder with her maw, her teeth piercing his rigid flesh. Alrick spun, grabbing her at her haunches and yanking her from his shoulder.

Whirling in a circle, he slammed her against a tree, snapping her spine before dropping her in the grass. His demon rose to the surface, and drool dripped from his fangs. His sole purpose for the past four centuries had been to rid the world of magic, and he yearned to tear her limb from limb. But as this she-wolf shifted into her human form, a blood-red stone attached to a chain glinted on her chest.

He had found the Thropynite.

## CHAPTER FIVE

Amber looked up from her computer as Luke peeked his head into her office. She knew that look. Closing the laptop, she raised her brows, urging him to spill whatever news he had.

He straightened and strolled into the room, shoving his hands into his pockets. "You look nice today." Did she detect relief in his voice?

Sure, she occasionally worked a closing shift at the bar and blew off showering to open the place at five a.m. the next day, but she used dry shampoo and applied an extra layer of deodorant when she did. Shifters had sensitive noses, and she knew better than to offend the pack…or attract the wrong kind of attention…with her bodily odors. Luke would be leaving soon for work, so what did he care how she looked?

"We've got a visitor in from the Houston pack, and I need you to show him the city today. Play tour guide."

She shook her head. "No time. The AC guy is coming in at noon, and we have another shipment from Abita arriving soon. Ask Macey to do it."

"She's working. I already talked to Chase. He'll handle the shipment and the AC repair."

Her nostrils flared as she blew out a breath. Yes, as a member of the alpha family, part of her job was to help entertain important visitors, especially since Luke's mate was a police detective and rarely had time, but it irked her to no end when he meddled in the bar's affairs. This was *her* domain, and if anyone was going to rearrange the schedules, it was her.

She folded her arms on her desk. "And who will man the bar while he's doing all that?"

"Kaci. I had Chase call her. She'll be here in an hour."

Her nails scraped across the wood as she curled her hands into fists. "I'm perfectly capable of juggling the schedule at *my* bar, Luke. You do realize Dad transferred the title to me, right?"

He flashed a sympathetic look that reminded her far too much of their mother's. "You're right, and I apologize for overstepping. Will you do this for me?"

"And here I thought you were coming in with news about Nylah."

"The congress hasn't returned my call."

"Did you talk to Dad? Maybe he can speed things along." Her feeling about Nylah had lessened since yesterday, the danger no longer seeming imminent. Now it felt downright strange, flitting in and out of her consciousness and making her wonder if the premonition was real or if it was brought on by Noah's strong connection to his twin and Amber's intense feelings for Noah. But she couldn't explain that to her brother.

"I did. You'll be the first to know when I hear something. I remember you were close…to both her and Noah." A funny look crossed his face when he mentioned

Noah, which meant their mother had spoken to him about her impending mating deadline. And that must've meant...

"Strange timing that we'd get an *important* visitor when a supernatural murderer is on the loose in the city. Did the congress send him?"

Luke shook his head, trying to look innocent and failing miserably. "He's just in town to see what our lovely city has to offer."

"Mm-hmm." She opened her desk drawer and pulled a tube of red lipstick and a mirror from her purse. "I suppose I should look my best to ensure he's impressed by what *our city* has to offer." She ran the lipstick in a circle around her mouth, letting it bleed well past her natural lip line. "And I'll be sure to smile." She caked on another layer before brushing it across her front teeth. "How's this, Brother?"

"Amber... C'mon, he'll be here in a couple of hours, and you look ridiculous." He pulled a tissue from the box on her desk and offered it to her.

She yanked it from his hand, but she didn't wipe her face. "I'm not an idiot. Mom and Dad sent him, didn't they?"

He sighed heavily. "You've only got six months to find a mate, and they know how picky you are. They're covering their bases."

She scoffed. "I'd have expected more from you, Luke. After everything you went through..." She scrubbed the lipstick from her teeth.

"I don't like it any more than you do, but Dad's on the congress now. What do you want me to do?"

"Next time, tell me about it so I can put a stop to it before the guy drives all this way. I'm not a piece of livestock to be bought or a prize to be won. I'm a werewolf, and I'll choose my own mate."

"As long as it's another werewolf." He winked. Of course he could joke about the antiquated law now; he got to mate with his fate-bound.

She rolled her eyes. "Yes, of course."

"Just take the guy to lunch. If he doesn't interest you, then send him on his way."

"I won't hesitate to." She gazed at the clown-like smile she'd drawn on her face and grimaced. *Way to act your age, Amber.* She'd played into the second-born, alpha's little sister role for far too long. She wasn't a damsel in distress, nor did she desire to be. It was time she started acting like the capable woman she was.

"I'll give him a chance, okay?" She set the mirror and tissue on the desk. "And I'll find a mate by my next birthday."

"That's all I ask." Luke smiled and turned to leave, but he paused and gestured to his face. "You might want to..."

"Yeah. I'll clean myself up."

In the bathroom, Amber redid her makeup and ran a brush through her hair before returning to her office to stew while she waited for her "date." She couldn't stay mad at Luke. Their mother was persistent at best, and whether or not Amber found a mate would affect him as well. She just wished her family trusted her to make the right decisions. She wasn't as helpless as they made her out to be, even if she acted like a child every now and then.

Fifteen minutes before John Wilkinson, a high-ranking shifter from the Houston pack, was due to arrive, she strolled into the bar and took a long drink from the beer Chase poured for her. Lord knew she'd need it to endure this. She could only imagine the type of man her father thought would be a suitable mate.

Twenty minutes later, a tall, beefy guy with a shaved head and hard-set eyes sauntered in. He squinted as his vision adjusted to the dim lighting, and Amber took in all six feet of him.

He wore jeans that stretched tight over his muscular thighs, and his biceps looked like they might bust through his shirt sleeves with the slightest flex. She was about to consider the "everything's bigger in Texas" motto when her gaze landed on a belt buckle the size of a dinner plate. *The bigger the buckle, the smaller the…*

He cleared his throat and addressed Chase, not even giving her a glance. "I'm here to meet the alpha's sister."

Chase fought a smile and looked at her.

"The alpha's sister has a name." She rotated her stool to face him, but she didn't bother standing up. "Do you know it?"

He scrunched his brow, looking annoyed that she'd spoken and also confused like he really couldn't recall it.

"I'm Amber Mason." She rose and offered her hand. "You must be John."

He raked his gaze up and down her body before taking her hand in a grip so light he must've thought she was made from porcelain. "Hmm." He cut his gaze toward the half-empty glass on the bar. "Are you drinking beer?" His tone held accusation, which made Amber bristle. She received enough judgment from her family. She didn't need it from this guy too.

"I am." She picked it up and took a giant gulp, her gaze never straying from his eyes.

The disgusted look on his face made it evident he didn't like women who drank beer, but he managed to pull a neutral expression as he said, "I'll join you," to her and then, "Give me your darkest brew," to Chase.

Amber chugged the rest of her beer and set the glass on the bar. "We should get going. I want to make it to the restaurant before the lunch rush." Because she could not stand to wait an hour for a table with this Neanderthal. Based on the two minutes she'd known him, it was obvious he was a controlling wannabe alpha. *So* not her type. What were her parents thinking?

John glanced between Amber and her empty glass before saying, "Let's go then."

She faked a smile and followed him into the sultry summer heat. The sun beat down on her from a cloudless sky as they made their way to The Court of Two Sisters for brunch.

They were seated near a front window at a table draped in white linen, and Amber pretended to peruse the menu while she waited for the waitress to arrive. She'd dined here so many times, she had it memorized, and her mouth watered at the thought of savoring her favorite dish.

Lifting her gaze, she stole a glance at John, her would-be mate, if her parents had their way. Actually, this setup had her father written all over it. She could see how a man like John would seem a perfect mate to someone as old school as her dad. He was strong and dominant, so he'd make a good protector. But as she tried to imagine some positive qualities in John, her mind drifted to thoughts of Noah.

If she were going to be superficial, Noah was ten times hotter than John. He was also kind, friendly, and smart. This guy hadn't smiled once, and she'd bet his giant belt buckle was compensating for more than the appendage below it.

*Stop it, Amber. You promised to give the guy a chance.* An ice cube's chance at staying cold in hell. She couldn't get her mind off Noah.

The waitress arrived to take their order, and as Amber opened her mouth to speak, John cut her off. "I'll have the steak and eggs, and the lady will have the yogurt parfait."

*Whoa, buddy.* Did he actually order for her? And the cheapest entrée available, while he got the most expensive?

"No. No, I won't." Amber handed the waitress her menu. "I'll have the shrimp and grits, please."

John frowned as the waitress walked away. "Do you eat like that all the time?"

"Do you always assume you know what your dates want to eat without asking them?" She arched a brow and sipped her water, staring at him over the rim of her glass.

"You'll need to watch your weight. I won't have my mate letting herself go."

"Letting herself—" She clamped her mouth shut. Her actions on this "date" affected more than herself. She was representing her pack, so she'd best get it together and make it through brunch without offending the man.

Clearing her throat, she straightened her spine and plastered on a fake smile. "How long are you in town for?"

"Just today. I leave first thing in the morning. My job is demanding but flexible. I can work from New Orleans."

"Mm-hmm." She feigned interest. "Where are you staying?"

"Your father put me up in the Hotel Monteleone."

"Nice." Of course he did.

Their food arrived, and John told her about his pack in Texas, his job, and his family, not once asking her a question about herself. "My alpha tendencies have caused some friction with leadership, so it'll be good for me to join a pack where I'll actually have some pull."

"I see." She shoveled a mound of grits into her mouth.

"We'll have two children. I prefer to only have one, but the second will be back-up in case the first doesn't survive. I must have a shifting offspring."

In case the first didn't survive? What did he think this was? District Twelve?

"Your hips are a good size for birthing, so I'm not concerned about that."

Birthing… She couldn't help but laugh. He was so far off from being anyone she would even consider taking as her mate.

He frowned. "Your laugh is too high-pitched. Werewolves have sensitive ears, so you'll have to work on toning it down."

She laughed louder, and his expression turned even more sour.

When they finished their meals, John paid the tab and looked into her eyes. "Do you prefer your house or my hotel room?"

"For what?" She had a feeling she knew exactly what for, but she wanted to hear him say it.

"Your father said you prefer a fate-bound mate. It's obvious that's not going to happen between us, and that's a sacrifice I'm willing to make. After some time with me in the bedroom, you'll be willing as well." He said it with a completely straight face, as if he actually believed he had a magic dick.

This time, she snorted when she laughed.

Noah sauntered alongside Cade down Royal Street, the midday sun nearly unbearable as he chugged the rest of his sweet tea and tossed the paper cup into a trash can. His friend wore shorts and a loose tank, much more suitable clothing for the Louisiana heat than Noah's jeans and heavy work boots. Sweat beaded on his forehead, dripping into his eyes as he stepped around a group of tourists gathering on the sidewalk.

"I'm glad you could get away on your lunch break." Cade swept a lock of blond hair off his forehead. "I haven't seen you in ages."

"Nearly a month." Noah continued his trek toward the building his crew was remodeling.

"I almost asked Luke for a job so I could make sure my buddy was really okay."

Noah laughed. "I bet that would have gone over well with your boss."

Cade shrugged. "He let me take the day off today. I could've finagled a few more 'mental health' days if I needed to. James assured me you were still alive though."

"Thanks for checking up on me." Noah's brow pinched. At least his buddy had inquired about him in his absence. "Amber didn't bother to ask." He clamped his mouth shut. His sulking was better done in privacy.

"You're still hung up on her? Have you seen her since your probation ended?"

He crossed the street to avoid the crowd watching a musician play the saxophone. Elegant music drifted on the air, and the spicy scent of boiling crawfish drifted out from a restaurant. "Yeah. She assumed I was spending all my time with a woman."

Cade clapped him on the shoulder. "Sounds to me like she didn't ask because she was jealous."

"Doubtful."

"Have you told her how you feel?"

"You know what happened when I tried."

"Damn." Cade stopped walking and peered into the window of The Court of Two Sisters. "I was going to suggest you try again, but this might be the reason why she wasn't concerned. Look."

Noah strode toward him, stopping in his tracks when he saw the view. Amber sat across from a barrel-chested male with a shaved head. She laughed so hard, she wiped a tear from her eye, and Noah's heart wrenched in his chest.

He huffed, turning on his heel and stomping away. Why the hell was he doing this to himself? She'd made it clear she wanted nothing more than friendship from him, yet he'd held on to a tiny spark of hope. Gods only knew why. As if he could actually awaken his dormant wolf with some made-up magic he read about online. *Get over it, man.*

"Hey, don't sweat it." Cade jogged to catch up. "If you mated with her, you'd have to deal with all the politics of being in the alpha family. That would be a pain in the ass."

"You're right. She's out of my league."

"That's not what I meant."

"Doesn't matter. I've got to get back to work."

"Let's go out tonight. With James mated and you on probation, I've had to fly solo the past month, and that's not nearly as fun. You wanna play wingman? Get your mind off things?"

Noah started to say "no," but a night out with Cade might be just what he needed. Lord knew he had to get over Amber as quickly as he could. She'd be mated within the next six months, and it wouldn't be to him.

## CHAPTER SIX

"Witches," Alrick growled low in his throat. He despised witches…detested them. Of all the magical beings he was created to eradicate, he loathed witches the most. Three hundred years in suspended animation could do that to a man.

A trio of the odious creatures strolled down Dauphine Street, laughing and carrying on as if they belonged in this wretched city. As if they deserved to live. He'd made the mistake of allowing one's existence to continue, and he had regretted it ever since. He wouldn't let it happen again. As soon as he regained his strength, he'd banish every last one of them from the face of the earth.

When they reached a pale green two-story with white trim and a wrought-iron balcony, the witches turned down St. Philip and disappeared through an alley entrance. Perfect. They'd secluded themselves so he could do his job in privacy.

"Oh, check out his costume. I want a picture." A human woman stumbled toward him before he could follow the witches, and Alrick curled his lip.

The strangeness of this city allowed him to be seen near the vile street they called Bourbon without causing alarm, but the inebriated lacked the inhibitions to stay away from danger. Their ignorance was maddening.

"Come on, babe. We'll get a picture tomorrow." At least her escort was in his right mind. He guided her away, and Alrick strode across the street to track the witches.

He grasped the handle of the green door that led into the alley, but he found it locked. No sound drifted toward him, which meant the revolting creatures had already ventured inside their dwelling. Good. This would offer him even more privacy to take his time and enjoy their demise.

With a shove, he wrenched the door open and slipped into the alley. A staircase scaled the side of the building, and a potted fern adorned the second-floor landing. He took the steps three at a time, inhaling deeply when he reached the top. The faint scent of witches, warm and herbal, assaulted his nostrils, and a tinge of something…other…lingered in the air. He couldn't place the supernatural aroma, but it didn't matter. He would eradicate New Orleans of *all* magic.

Ramming his shoulder against the door, he busted it open and stormed into a small living room. One woman screamed, and a man scrambled to the opposite end of the sofa, while the second woman lunged for a bottle on a shelf.

She uncorked it and chanted a spell. What magic she believed would stop a gargoyle, he didn't know, and he almost paused to witness her display of power before he killed her. But the other witch's screams had surely alerted the neighbors to his presence, so he grasped her neck, snapping her vertebrae in his grip and crushing her trachea.

The man lunged, but Alrick simply swung his arm, his stone-like fist shattering his skull and sending him careening to the floor. His mouth watered, the demon inside him screaming for sustenance, so he lifted the dying man from the floor and plunged his talons into his chest, ripping out his heart.

"Jasper!" the witch wailed and dropped to her knees.

Alrick snarled and threw the bloodied, limp body across the room. It crashed through the window and tumbled head over feet to the sidewalk below.

"Look what you made me do, enchantress." Alrick's anger seethed, the memory of another witch's betrayal fueling the fire in his blackened soul. He lunged for her, biting into her neck and severing the pulsing artery. Blood sprayed from the wound, and she gurgled, sucking in a dying breath.

As she lay on the floor, bleeding out, Alrick consumed the man's heart. He shivered as the organ slid down his throat, and he closed his eyes, allowing himself a moment to bask in the feel of his body being restored.

But the shouts of panic from outside interrupted his pleasure. Law enforcement would swarm the apartment soon, and he hadn't yet gained the strength to withstand their weapons. He plunged his talons into the women's chests, taking their hearts, and silently slipped out the door before rushing down the stairs and escaping in a flash of magic.

"What about those two?" Cade tipped his beer bottle toward a pair of blondes at the bar, but all Noah saw was an image of Amber's face as she laughed at whatever the shifter she was dating had said. It had been ages since he'd seen her laugh that hard, and the thought of another man bringing her so much joy gnawed in his gut like termites in an abandoned wood shack, eating away at him from the inside out.

A band took the stage and played a smooth jazz tune, and Noah cast his gaze toward the bar. Rows of liquor bottles lined the shelves, and a massive mirror hung above them, reflecting the revelry in the room. People smiled and laughed, but Noah couldn't stop his frown.

He set his half-empty beer on the table. He should've been happy for Amber. He *was* happy for her. Well, at least he would try to be. "Sorry, man. I'm not feeling it tonight."

Cade sighed as two men approached the ladies he'd set his sights on. "Yeah. Neither am I. You wanna jet?"

Noah nodded and headed for the door. When they reached the sidewalk, a hawker holding a sign that read *Big Ass Beer* shouted at them, motioning for them to enter the club across the street. Noah ignored the man and hung a right, but he cut across the street to avoid passing in front of the strip club where his trouble began. Two extra bouncers stood outside with the women, and he recognized the one who'd pinned him to the wall. He wouldn't be going anywhere near that place for a while…if ever again.

Thick clouds blanketed the dark sky, and the sweltering summer air clung to his skin like a wet electric blanket. The crowds of Bourbon Street thinned the deeper into the Quarter they ventured, the clubs and shops giving way to residences with window baskets overflowing with flowers. Here, the night felt peaceful, but as they made their way toward St. Philip Street, a blood-curdling scream pierced the night.

"Holy shit! Call 911." A man pulled the screaming woman to his chest and took his phone from his pocket.

Instinct drew Noah toward the commotion, but he hesitated. His protective nature was what had landed him on probation last month, and he wasn't about to make that mistake again. Cade didn't falter. He picked up the pace, striding toward Dauphine Street as if he were the police himself.

"Oh, hell." Noah jogged to catch up. Instinct was impossible to fight for long. "Need some help, folks?" he asked as he approached the couple, but the last word got stuck in his throat.

A man lay on the sidewalk in front of a pale green two-story, his lifeless eyes frozen wide in shock, a gaping, bloody hole in his chest where his heart should have been. *Not again.*

"Son of a bitch. I know him." Cade fisted his hands and tilted his head up to sift through the scents in the air.

"Who is he?" Noah asked.

"His name's Jasper. He's a second-born from the Biloxi pack, studying at Tulane. I've hung out with him a couple of times."

"This makes four," Noah said under his breath. A crowd began to form around the body, and sirens blared in the distance. "We've got to go."

Cade's jaw ticked as he ground his teeth. "It's personal now."

"Come on." Noah grabbed his arm. The last thing he

needed was to be caught by the human police with a victim from the same murderer. "Let's go find the bastard."

Cade nodded, lifting his nose again as they strode away from the fray. "Do you smell that?"

Noah inhaled deeply, and the faintest scent of rotting garbage reached his senses. "Either someone threw out some rancid meat, or we've got a demon on our hands."

"It gets stronger this way." Cade took off down St. Philip, and Noah followed.

They zig-zagged through the streets of the French Quarter, the scent of demon intensifying in some areas and then dissipating as they moved toward it.

"It's like the bastard disappears," Noah said. "He's not leaving a trail."

"Some demons can do that. They teleport." Cade motioned for Noah to follow him down Burgundy. "If this guy has that kind of magic, it means he's a strong one."

Strong enough to rip the hearts from his victims and disappear without a trace. The pack had their work cut out for them this time. They caught another whiff of demon scent, and as they followed it toward St. Louis Cemetery Number One, a sinking sensation formed in the pit of Noah's stomach. It had been weeks since Nylah's last text. What if she had met the same fate as Jasper, but no one had found her body?

No, he refused to entertain the idea. He had to focus on the issue at hand, which was the fact that their noses had led them straight to the city of the dead.

"What is it with monsters always hiding out in the cemetery?" Noah pulled a file from his pocket, which he always kept on hand for situations like this, and picked the lock. He and Cade slipped inside, and he shut the gate behind them, setting the lock so it looked closed to anyone who might walk by.

They paused at the entrance, listening for any signs of movement within the stone walls. Row after row of aboveground graves created a maze inside the single square-block cemetery, with multiple generations of New Orleanians entombed in each one. Some were well taken care of, with pristine white plaster and flowers adorning the façades, while others appeared weathered, the brick and mortar exposed to the elements after years of neglect.

"That's a new one." Cade nodded toward a massive gargoyle sitting a few yards away.

Noah peered at it through the darkness. If he didn't know any better, he'd say it had blood running down its chin. "It's old enough for mildew stains. Look at its face."

"True," Cade said. "Guess I haven't been here in a while. Meet you in ten?"

"Howl if you find anything."

Cade slipped between a row of tombs and shifted into his wolf, while Noah strode in the opposite direction, weaving between the graves. The rancid scent of demon was strong, so the fiend had at least been here recently, if he wasn't still inside. Noah's half of the cemetery turned up no results, but as he made his way toward the entrance, something felt off. He turned in a circle, taking in his surroundings.

The gargoyle was gone.

A grunt sounded behind him, and Noah spun to find what he'd mistaken as a statue rising to its full height and smelling of fiend. Before he could shout for Cade, the demon planted both hands against Noah's chest, shoving him backward into a tomb. His head hit the brick with a smack, and his vision swam.

Cade barreled in with his teeth bared and plowed toward the demon. The fiend grunted again, taking off in the opposite direction, and Noah scrambled to his feet to give chase. He ran after Cade, but the wolf stopped abruptly, jerking his head around with his ears pricked.

Noah froze, listening, but the demon didn't give away his location. He crept down one aisle, while Cade prowled another. He turned, going up another row and down the next. When they met in the center of the cemetery, Cade shifted to human, his wolf's body shimmering with magic as he transformed.

"The bastard disappeared." Cade pulled his phone from his pocket. "I'll call Luke. You let Macey know the cops were called."

"I'm on it." Noah dialed her number and said a silent prayer to whatever gods might be listening that, wherever she was, Nylah wouldn't cross paths with this fiend.

## CHAPTER SEVEN

Amber sat in a green vinyl chair next to Noah in Luke's office. It was six a.m., and the citrusy scent of his shampoo still lingered in his hair. She leaned on the arm of the chair, drifting closer to him and breathing in his intoxicating scent.

Her mating instincts must've been kicking in hard. Noah had always smelled good, but damn. She wanted to wrap herself up and get lost in him…unlike the Neanderthal her father had set her up with yesterday.

She'd managed to rein in her laughter and politely inform him that sex would not change her mind about the pairing, but he'd left New Orleans none too pleased. Once word spread of her rejecting such a "viable male," no doubt the race would be on to see who could win her hand. Wouldn't that be fun? *No, not really.*

Noah looked at her, arching a brow in question, and she realized she was leaning way too close to him. She sat up straight, and her head spun like it always did when her empathic premonitions were about to reveal themselves. Clutching the arms of the chairs, she braced herself for the ominous feeling about Nylah to slam into her psyche, but it didn't come.

This premonition was about Noah. *Change.* Something about him was going to change. She dug in deep, settling into the feeling and hoping against hope that her ability would reveal more.

It didn't.

She blew out a hard breath. Leave it to her to have a gut feeling about the one man she could imagine spending her life with, yet all her ability told her was "change."

"Are you okay?" Noah's gaze held concern. "Did you get something more on Nylah?"

"No." She rubbed her chest. "I think it's heartburn." There was no point in sharing what she'd just felt about him. Change could come in so many forms. Maybe it simply meant their relationship would finally turn back to normal. He'd been acting strangely around her well before his probation, and it was time she got to the bottom of it.

"The full moon is tomorrow," she said. "Will you be joining us this time?"

Indecision tightened his eyes as he held her gaze, and the tendons in his neck tensed like he was grinding his teeth.

Why was he acting so weird? "It's a simple yes or no question."

"Yeah. Yeah, of course I'll be there." He straightened. "Why wouldn't I be?"

She narrowed her eyes. "What's going on?"

"What do you mean?"

She gestured from herself to him. "This awkwardness between us. Where is it coming from?"

He let out a nervous laugh. "I've been gone for nearly a month, and you thought I'd abandoned you, so…"

"No, this started before all that. A few months before, actually. If it's because I started flirting with you, I'm sorry."

He blinked, missing a beat in his reply. "When did you start flirting with me?"

"Well, I didn't, but I wanted to until you got all weird. I thought maybe I'd flirted by accident with the way you've been acting."

"Why would…?" He clamped his mouth shut and shook his head. "*I* started to flirt with *you*, and you shot me down, so I backed off."

"When did I shoot you down?"

His brow rose like he couldn't believe what he was hearing. Honestly, she couldn't believe it herself. "You said you were glad we were friends because you knew I wasn't after you for your pack status. I know when I've been relegated to the friendzone."

"Relegat—" She huffed. "That's not what I meant by that."

"Sure sounded like it." He cast his gaze to the wall in front of him.

Amber chewed the inside of her cheek and stared at his profile. He had a strong jawline, with coarse auburn hair peppering his skin. He closed his eyes for a long blink, and the air conditioner hummed as the fan kicked on, filling the room with cool air.

"Noah…" She clutched his hand. "I meant that as a compliment. I thought we were becoming more than friends, and I meant I was glad I could trust you. That I could date you without having to worry that you only wanted me to give you an alpha child."

His lips twitched like he was having trouble forming the right words.

"Why didn't you say anything?" she asked.

"Probably for the same reason you didn't ask about me when I was gone. Wounded pride." He shook his head and leaned away from her. "It doesn't matter. You seemed happy with the guy you had lunch with yesterday. Is he going to be your mate?"

*Jesus, word travels fast.* "How did you know about that?"

"I saw you through the window, laughing. He must be a funny guy. I'm happy for you."

"Are you?" She bit her bottom lip. If anything, he seemed jealous. "Noah, I was laughing *at* him, not with him. He was half-cowboy/half-caveman. I sent him packing as soon as I could."

The door swung open, and she jerked her hand back into her lap.

"I'll make this quick," Luke said as he strode into the office and sat behind his desk. "We're behind at the jobsite, and we need to head there immediately."

Noah straightened, lowering his gaze slightly, showing respect for the alpha. Amber leaned forward in her chair.

"The body you and Cade found last night wasn't the only one. There were two more in the apartment above."

"Christ," Noah said. "Any of ours?"

Luke shook his head. "Witches again. Until this is resolved, no non-shifters are allowed on the streets in the Quarter after dark, Noah and Macey excluded." He looked at Amber. "Are we clear?"

She nodded. "What did you learn about Nylah?"

"She missed her last check-in," Luke said. "The congress hasn't heard from her in a week."

Amber's stomach sank. While the feeling of impending doom for Nylah had passed, something still felt off about her. Like she was out of danger for now…or the threat had already come and passed…but she was standing on a slippery slope.

"Do they know where she might be?" Noah asked. "Where was she when she last checked in?"

"She was in Mississippi last month," Luke said. "After they read the report of the murder you discovered, she was ordered to New Orleans. She hasn't made contact since."

Amber looked at Noah. "Have your parents heard from her? Surely she'd at least contact them if she was in town."

Noah started to answer, but Luke cut him off. "They haven't, and that's no surprise. National agents are forbidden from contacting anyone in their pack."

"Why was she sent here?" Amber asked. "We've never needed the congress to get involved with supernatural policing."

Luke shook his head. "No, we haven't, but this is where things get weird. She was sent to investigate the reappearance of the Grunch."

Noah cocked his head. "I thought that was nothing more than an urban legend."

"Me too," Amber added. "It was made up by kids as an excuse to scare their friends. You drive down Grunch Road, and if you see a goat, the cannibal dwarves will come out and eat you."

"I thought it was an urban legend as well, but the congress assures me it's not. After the demon Noah and Cade encountered last night, I believe it." Luke opened his laptop and punched a few keys. "The Grunch are human-demon hybrid abominations created by a European religious sect centuries ago. They fused demon souls with an army of human warriors and used a magical crystal called

Thropynite to give them shifting abilities. They transformed into gargoyle-like creatures—like the fiend you and Cade encountered—and swept through towns and villages, murdering magical beings."

"Are you serious?" she asked.

Luke nodded. "A group of them somehow made it to New Orleans, and that's where the Grunch legend began. No one has seen hide nor tail of them in centuries, but it looks like something woke them."

Amber glimpsed Noah from the corner of her eye, and he'd gone pale.

"Thropynite is real…" He stared straight ahead, not seeming to focus on anything for a moment before he blinked and shook his head. "I've heard stories about it, but I thought it was legend too."

"It was destroyed more than one hundred years ago," Luke said, "but someone stole a sizeable shard and has been selling pieces on the black market. If some made it to the US, it could have awakened the creatures who came here centuries ago."

"Holy crap." Amber slumped in her seat.

"Tell me about it," Luke said.

"We need to find the Grunch. They must have my sister." Noah fisted his hands on his lap, and Amber placed her hand on top of his.

"Her trouble might not even be related to that. I haven't had any feelings connecting the two, so she might just be indisposed. Whatever it is, we'll find her; won't we, Luke?" She shot her brother a hard look.

"If we are dealing with the gargoyle shifters, they only operate at night." He looked at Noah. "I want you and Cade to head to the Grunch Road area at sundown to see what you can find."

"I'll go with them. She's my friend too."

"No, you will not." Luke arched a brow at her. "Noah and Macey are the only non-shifters with permission to patrol."

She straightened her spine. "Then don't call it patrolling. Call it looking for my friend."

"As your alpha, I forbid it." His gaze softened. "And as your brother, I'm asking you nicely not to. Please, Amber. They've already killed one second-born. I won't risk it happening to you."

She pursed her lips, glancing at Noah before returning her gaze to Luke. She'd concede this time. Her second-born ability wasn't intended for fighting, and her presence could put Noah and Cade at risk if they felt like they had to protect her…which they would. They all treated her like she was fragile, and that irked her to no end. "All right. But keep me posted."

"You do the same if you get any more details from your premonitions." He stood and motioned to the door. "Let's get to work."

Amber rose and touched Noah's arm. "I'll see you tomorrow night, right?"

He nodded absently. "Yeah. I'll be here."

---

Noah parked his Chevy along the side of Grunch Road and killed the engine before sliding out of the truck and closing the door. Cade and James joined him near the ditch, and all three men stared up at the nearly full moon. A wispy patch of clouds stretched across it, the light giving it a silvery glow against the inky sky, and the summer air was warm and muggy against his skin.

James, the senior shifter and lead wolf on the demon-hunting team, jerked his head toward the trees, indicating they should follow him into the woods. Dead leaves and twigs crunched beneath Noah's boots as he paced behind the two shifters. The atmosphere felt thicker in this part of the swamp, almost as if he could slice it open and get lost inside.

"It's quiet," Noah said. "Do y'all ever hunt out here?"

"Never," James said. "This place has bad energy. Even Odette was worried about us coming out here."

"I'm surprised she let you," Cade said with a wink, which earned him an irritated glare.

"My mate communes with the spirit of death. When she has a concern, I listen to her."

Cade chuckled, running a hand through his short blond hair as he turned to Noah. "Have I told you how glad I am to have you back? This old geezer would rather stay home than go out anymore."

"Someday, when you find your fate-bound, you'll understand," James said.

Noah faked a laugh. "At least I'll never have to worry about having a ball and chain that heavy."

Cade clapped him on the shoulder. "Lucky you."

*Yeah, right.* His friends had no idea how badly he wanted the ability to have a fate-bound. Especially after his last conversation with Amber. Luke had interrupted them before they could finish, but that was probably for the best. Noah could never be the werewolf she needed… that she deserved…but he had to admit learning she might have feelings for him sent a thrill rushing through his veins.

Hell, it was more than a thrill. Amber reached all the way to his soul.

They trudged deeper into the woods, until Cade lifted a hand and stopped. "This is where the Grunch supposedly lived. Are your Wonder Twin powers picking up on anything? Can you sense Nylah?"

Closing his eyes, Noah sucked in a deep breath and opened his senses. The energy around him pricked at his skin, palpable and thick. But aside from the foreboding pressure in the air and the low vibration giving the area its bad vibe, he felt nothing. Nylah wasn't there.

He tugged a flashlight from his pocket and shined the beam into the clearing. "Y'all go do your thing. I'll have a look around here and see what I can find."

"We'll meet back in fifteen," James said before calling on his magic and shifting into his wolf. Dark gray fur rolled down the length of his massive body, and as his front paws hit the ground, he took off running.

"See ya on the flip side." Cade shifted and followed James, bounding deeper into the swamp and leaving Noah alone with the sickening thoughts that had plagued him since Luke mentioned the Thropynite.

From the moment Noah turned thirteen and his wolf gene failed to activate, Nylah had become obsessed with finding a way to unlock it for him. She felt guilty being the only shifting wolf when they should have shared the magic, and she'd gone to great lengths, trying numerous experiments to reverse the outcome of his delayed birth.

When the local witches couldn't cast a spell to help him, she'd scoured the dark web, consulting with black magic practitioners to find a way to change Noah's fate. But when fate dealt your hand, you had no choice but to play the cards you were given.

In her research, she'd come across the legend of the Thropynite. Supposedly, if a non-shifting were held a piece, the stone would activate their dormant gene, awakening the wolf inside them. She and Noah made a pact that they would do everything they could to find it.

In her absence—or maybe before she left—Nylah must have learned of its actual existence. That was what her cryptic texts were about. It was the only explanation.

Noah grunted, switching off his flashlight and returning it to his pocket. If she got her hands on a piece of Thropynite, that would certainly be the answer to his prayers. But there was no telling what kind of trouble she might have gotten herself into trying to obtain it. Black market dealings were shady at best, downright deadly at worst, and if she'd used her status as a spy for the national congress to obtain it, she could be looking at threats from both sides.

He'd never forgive himself if he was the reason Nylah was in danger. And if the Grunch really had awakened because the Thropynite was here, then he and Nylah were to blame for the recent murders. *Holy hell.*

He sent a text to the last number she'd messaged him from, but he got no reply, not that he expected one. Every text she sent had come from a different number. No doubt they were burner phones, which she discarded frequently to avoid being traced.

Footsteps sounded to his left, and Noah dragged out the flashlight again, shining it into the trees where Cade and James approached in human form.

"Nothing out of the ordinary," Cade said. "Did you find anything?"

A crack in a thick trunk drew Noah's attention to the right, and he strode toward the tree. "Check this out."

The ground beneath the branches had been disturbed recently, the grass flattened to indicate something had been dragged a short distance. James ran his hand along the trunk, peeling away a piece of loose bark as he examined the damage.

"Some kind of fight happened here," he said before he straightened and angled his nose upward to catch the breeze. "It could've been anything. Bobcats, boar…hell, even gators venture this far onto dry land sometimes."

"Yeah, and I know Nylah," Cade said. "She'd have put up a helluva fight if she were in trouble, so she either won this scuffle, or it wasn't her."

"You're right." Noah jerked his head toward his truck and trudged back to the road. Nylah was tough; she could take care of herself. He wouldn't have been worried about her at all if not for Amber's initial empathic premonition of trouble.

And a nagging feeling in the back of his mind said he was the reason for all of it.

# CHAPTER EIGHT

Amber glanced at the clock and drummed her fingers on the bar. Where the hell was Noah? She'd convinced Kaci to come in early and cover her shift, and now the man had the nerve to stand her up after their conversation was cut short yesterday morning? *So not cool.*

Her feelings for Noah weren't just bubbling to the surface; they'd reached a full-blown boil, and she'd be damned if she'd let a miscommunication come between them again.

She'd been thinking about it all day, rolling every scenario she could imagine around in her mind, and they all led to one conclusion. She needed to be up front with Noah. Just lay it all out, tell him how she felt, and demand…in a nice way…that he be honest about where they stood. What did she have to lose?

Her best friend, for one thing. But keeping her feelings for him bottled up was eroding her psyche from the inside out. It was best to rip off the duct tape and spill it all. If he didn't feel the same and their friendship didn't survive, then it wasn't as rock-solid as she thought.

"Are you okay?" Her sister-in-law, Macey, rested a hand on top of hers, stilling her incessant drumming. "You're lucky your nails are short, or you'd have dug holes in the bar by now."

Amber bit her lip and fisted her hand. "Why don't men say what's on their minds? Why do they make assumptions and then shut down?"

Macey laughed. "I think they probably ask the same questions about women."

"I guess you're right."

"Noah?"

She looked at the clock again. "He should be here by now. I think I scared him off."

"He doesn't seem like the type to scare easily." Macey swiveled in her seat to face her, resting an elbow on the bar. "What happened?"

"We were talking yesterday morning before our meeting with Luke, and he—" Amber's gaze snapped toward the door as Noah sauntered in. He wore jeans with a tight gray t-shirt, looking sexy as hell.

One corner of his mouth lifted into a crooked smile as he caught her gaze, and she willed her frantically beating heart to slow. All but one lock of his auburn hair fell perfectly into place, the errant strand curving down across his forehead, drawing her attention to his deep brown eyes. *Damn.* The lid was off the pot, and she was boiling over.

"Not scared after all." Macey gave her a conspiratorial wink before sipping her beer.

As Noah made his way toward Amber, she slid off her stool and met him halfway across the floor. She needed to start this conversation as soon as possible, before she chickened out, and here in the bar, with a dozen second-borns and non-were mates as witnesses, was not the place to do it.

"Hey." His smile widened as she approached.

"Let's get out of here." As she clutched his hand, his magical energy joined with hers, shimmying up her arm and hitting her heart with a jolt. She froze, her head spinning as the feeling of change for Noah that she'd felt this morning intensified.

His brow furrowed. "Everything okay?"

Something was about to change as soon as she confessed her feelings. Hopefully it would be for the better. She shook her head to chase away the dizzying sensation the premonition caused. "Yeah. We haven't hung out in forever, so I thought we could grab a six-pack and head to the park."

He hesitated, glancing at the bar before looking into her eyes. "Okay. My truck's two blocks away. I'll drive."

They stopped by a convenience store to pick up some Blue Moon beer before heading toward City Park. She smiled as he stopped in the lot and slid out of the truck. She'd only said, "the park," yet he'd known the exact place she meant. How many times had they come out here as teens, lounging beneath the massive oaks, drinking beer Amber had swiped from the storeroom when her mom and dad ran the bar?

Noah opened the door and grinned. "What?"

"I was thinking about the time Nylah bumped me with her shoulder. She didn't know her own strength yet, and if you hadn't used your power to catch me, I'd have fallen into the lake." She stepped out of the truck and shut the door.

He shook his head. "Yeah, but I couldn't control it, remember? I threw you back into the bramble. By the time we untangled you from the mess, you were seething."

"I wasn't *that* mad."

He laughed. "Yes, you were."

"Okay, I was." But she got over it. She could never stay mad at Noah.

They made their way to an arched stone bridge and stood at the top, overlooking the stream below. Noah opened a beer and handed it to her before getting one for himself and clinking the can against hers.

"We've had some good times out here, haven't we?" he asked.

"We have." She turned around, resting her back against the railing. He stood next to her, still facing the water, close enough that she could smell his woodsy, masculine scent. Her stomach fluttered, and a slight nauseating sensation rolled through her core.

"Noah, I wanted to talk to you…" She looked at him, and he rubbed his chest, his face pinching with pain. "Are you okay?"

He rolled his shoulders, stretching his neck. "I'm fine. What did you want to talk about?"

"Us."

He raised his brow. "What about us?"

"Yesterday, you said I'd relegated you to the friendzone."

"Ah." He turned around, matching her posture. "It's okay. Really."

"It's not though. I don't want you to be in the friendzone." She held her breath, anticipating his response.

"Well." He blew out a hard breath before taking a swig

of beer. Then he opened his mouth like he wanted to say something, but he clamped it shut again.

She'd officially ripped off the duct tape. She might as well keep the confession flowing. "My feelings for you have changed, Noah. I can't be near you without my stomach fluttering; I think about you all the time when we're apart. I'm falling for you…for my best friend. Is that crazy?"

He set his beer can on the railing and faced her. "Amber…"

The fluttering in her stomach rose to her chest, coming out as something between a sob and a laugh. She should have kept her mouth shut. It was months ago when he thought she shut him down. He'd probably gotten over it and moved on. It was stupid of her to think, after all these years, their feelings for each other would bloom at the same time.

She nodded and set her can next to his. "It's okay. If you're not falling for me too, just tell me. We'll go back to being friends, and we can pretend like this conversation never happened."

He held her gaze, and a strange look formed in his eyes. "I'm not falling for you."

Her breath caught, and she swallowed the lump that crept into her throat. "Okay." That six-month deadline seemed a lot more ominous all of a sudden.

He tucked her hair behind her ear before resting his hand on her shoulder. "I fell a long time ago, and I never got back up."

Her heart couldn't decide if it wanted to stop or beat right out of her chest. Her best friend had fallen for her, and she for him. Pressure built in the back of her eyes, her throat thickening as another sob-laugh threatened to escape. "Why didn't you say something sooner? You know what? It doesn't matter." She took his face in her hands and kissed him.

He froze for a moment, and she almost pulled away. But before she could chide herself for jumping the gun, he slid his arms around her waist and kissed her back. A low moan escaped his throat as he tugged her tighter against his body, and when he coaxed her lips apart with his tongue, she couldn't help but lean into him and revel in the feel of his embrace.

*That wasn't so hard, was it?* She glided her hands over his shoulders and down his back, memorizing the way his muscles felt beneath her palms. His body was warm and hard in all the right places, and the coarseness of the scruff on his face contrasted with the softness of his lips.

He slipped his hand beneath the back of her shirt, and though it was rough from work, his touch was a gentle caress. With a deep inhale, he gripped her hips, first pressing his pelvis into hers and then gently pushing her away. "We can't do this."

She touched her fingers to her swollen lips. The taste of him lingered on her tongue, and she wanted more. "Should we head back to the truck?"

"No, I…" He raked a hand through his hair before fisting his hands on the bridge railing and staring up at the full moon. "I mean we can't do *us*."

"Did I move too fast? I figured, since we know each other so well, we didn't need to wait for our second date to kiss." She let out a nervous laugh, trying to lighten the mood.

He gripped the edge of the railing so tight his knuckles turned white. "Don't get me wrong. That kiss was amazing. *You* are amazing, but I can't… You shouldn't waste your time with me."

"Who says I would be wasting my time?"

"I do. Everyone would if we started dating. You were right when you said I wasn't interested in your alpha blood, but your alpha blood is the reason *you* shouldn't be interested in me."

"I don't understand." Well, really, she knew exactly what he was getting at, but she wanted to hear the words from him. Surely he didn't believe what he was hinting.

"You should mate with a shifting wolf."

*Damn.* He believed it. "Tell me why you think that."

"You know why, Amber."

She shook her head, lifting one shoulder in a dismissive shrug. "No, I don't. Please explain to me why you think you…or anyone else…knows whom I should mate with better than me." The words came out sharper than she'd intended, but she was done hiding her irritation about this subject. Noah, of all people, should have understood that.

"Your firstborn will be a shifting wolf who will hold rank in the pack. He should have at least one shifting parent."

"Oh, so you're saying you're not wolf enough to make up for my inadequacies. Is that it? That I won't be a good mother without a shifter telling me how to raise my kid? Do you hear yourself?"

"That's…" He winced and rubbed his chest. "No, that's not what I'm saying."

"What are you saying then? I'm listening."

"You deserve a fate-bound. That's something I can never be for you. I wish I could. I'd give my soul to be able to shift, but since my wolf is dormant, I... You deserve more."

"The only person who feels this way is you. Even my mother asked about you the other day, dropping a not-so-subtle hint that you would make a good mate. So if there's something else, you should say so because I'm not buying what you're selling."

"Don't you want to experience that kind of unconditional love? Isn't it worth waiting for?"

"I see. Now you're saying you can't love me unconditionally without magic sealing our fates. Plenty of people —werewolves included—find their happily ever afters without a fate-bound."

"I know. You're right..."

"And I'll tell you something else since we're on the subject of fate-bounds. *I* would never take a shifter as my mate unless his wolf claimed me, and guess what? I know every shifter in the pack, and not one of them has had even an inkling of a bond forming with me...not even the caveman my dad set me up with. I refuse to take away a shifter's chance at finding his fate-bound. They're all more interested in my status than my good looks and charming personality anyway."

He grinned. "You're awfully cute when you get on a roll like this. You always have been."

She narrowed her eyes. "No one—not you, not Luke, and especially not my mom or dad—is going to tell me whom I should be with. I will mate with a werewolf before my thirtieth birthday because I have to, but that were does *not* have to be a shifter. It probably won't be, but if you still think I'd be wasting my time by dating you, then say so now."

"You are—" He doubled over, clutching his stomach and groaning.

"Noah?" She gripped his shoulders. "What's wrong?"

"I don't know." As he straightened, he swayed, knocking his hip against the rail and nearly tumbling over into the water below.

Amber grabbed his arm, tugging him back onto the bridge. "Is it your stomach? Your head? Tell me what I can do."

"It's everything. It's…oh god." He doubled over again, this time landing on his hands and knees.

"Noah!" She knelt beside him, resting her hand on his back as he heaved in a breath. "I'm calling an ambulance."

"No." He shook his head. "No ambulance."

"Can you walk to the truck? We need to get you checked out." She tried to help him to his feet, but he waved her away.

"I don't think this is a medical issue." He groaned, digging his nails into the concrete.

"What is it then? A spell? A curse? Talk to me!"

"I don't know!" He coughed hard. "I don't know what's happening."

"I'm calling Alexis." She tugged her phone from her pocket and dialed the pack's healer, her hand trembling as she pressed the device to her ear. "Please pick up. Please pick up."

She answered on the third ring. "Hello?"

"It's Amber. There's something wrong with Noah. Can you come to the stone bridge in City Park?"

"What's going on?"

"I don't know. He's on his hands and knees on the ground, groaning, and he said it doesn't feel like a medical issue. Maybe it's a spell? Can you bring Rain too?" Chase's mate, Rain, was a witch who'd recently helped undo a spell that had wiped another werewolf's memory. Surely between her and Alexis, they could fix whatever was wrong with Noah.

"Put the phone on speaker so I can talk to him."

She did as Alexis asked and held the phone toward him, her heart wrenching as Noah let out another groan.

"I need you to describe how you're feeling," Alexis said. "What kind of pain is it?"

"It burns," he said through clenched teeth. "It's like acid in my veins."

"Amber, check his eyes. Are they dilated?"

"Noah, can you look at me?" She placed her hand on the side of his neck and lowered her head to meet his gaze. "They're constricted like pinpricks."

"Oh, shit," Alexis said.

"Oh, shit? What's 'oh, shit'? Don't say that." Panic raced ice-cold through her veins. "What's happening to him?"

"Can you get him in the car? You need to take him to the hunting grounds. Now."

"Why?" She tugged Noah up by the arm. "Walk with me. C'mon, you can do this." With his arm slung over her shoulders, she carried most of his weight as they trudged to his truck. He moaned, tripping over his own feet and nearly sending them both face-first into the dirt. She practically dragged him the rest of the way.

"Alexis, what's going on?" Amber helped him into the passenger seat before darting around to the driver's side and climbing in.

"Constricted pupils, doubling over in pain, blood that feels like acid… It sounds exactly like what happened to

Bryce before his first shift. Apparently, the pain is normal if the wolf awakens later in life."

She started the engine and stared blankly out the front window. "Noah can't shift."

"It sure as hell sounds like he's about to, and if you don't take him to the alpha, you might end up his first meal."

CHAPTER NINE

Nausea churned in Noah's stomach, an intense burning sensation pulsing through his body with each beat of his heart. He clutched the door handle as Amber sped down the highway, and he squeezed his eyes shut to ease the pounding in his head.

"Are you okay?" Amber reached across the seat to take his hand.

"No," he ground out through teeth clenched so hard he tasted blood.

"Alexis thinks you're getting ready to shift."

"I heard." He moved in the seat to rest his head against the window, hoping the cool glass would tame the fever threatening to burn him from the inside out. "It's impossible."

Amber winced and returned her hand to the steering wheel. "There is a way," she whispered.

Noah groaned. She was right; there was a way, but in his current state of agony, he couldn't add mental anguish to the pain.

"If Nylah…" She swallowed hard.

"I know." If a first-born shifting wolf died prematurely, the second-born's magic would be triggered, enabling them to shift. It was like a supernatural failsafe to ensure the pack had enough shifters.

He clenched his hands in his lap, pressing his feet into the floorboard and lifting his butt from the seat as his muscles contracted. "Can you drive any faster?" Whatever was happening to him, it was about to reach critical mass.

"We're almost there." She turned onto a side road.

His stomach lurched, and he bent over, pressing his head into the dashboard as he groaned. This couldn't be happening. He refused to believe Nylah was gone, yet he couldn't deny the intense pull of the moon. With every breath he took, he felt the magic growing stronger until his entire body began to hum—no…to vibrate.

The truck bounced as Amber pulled off the path and rolled to a stop. "I'm sure Alexis will be here soon." She rubbed his back, trying to console him, but her hand on his body felt like an electric shock, setting his nerves on fire.

"Ah, fuck." The vibration in his muscles intensified, the burning acid in his veins melting his insides. Every nerve in his body screamed with pain as if he were being shredded into ten million pieces. It was happening. "Get out of the car."

"Noah…"

"You heard Alexis. I don't want to hurt you." His body seized, the magic consuming him. "Run."

Amber's breath hitched, and she reached a trembling hand toward the latch before sliding out of the truck. "I'm here for you, Noah. I know you won't hurt me."

"I don't," he forced out a moment before his wolf came to life.

Amber froze, staring in awe at the magnificent creature lying in the seat. Copper fur covered his body, with a sprinkling of black across his shoulders, and Noah's brown eyes gazed back at her. "You're beautiful," she whispered.

Shifters retained their human thoughts and emotions in wolf form. While he couldn't speak, he would understand her. His fur looked so soft, she couldn't help herself. She reached a hand toward him, and his lips peeled back, revealing white teeth with a massive set of canines.

She gasped and jerked her hand away. "Why don't you come out of the truck?"

A growl rumbled in his chest as he rose to his paws. He lowered his head in what looked like a predatory stance, but he was so big he would have hit the ceiling otherwise. He wasn't growling at *her*. He couldn't be.

Still, she took a few steps back, moving out of the way just in case. When his growl turned into a snarl, her heart slammed against her chest.

He leaped from the truck, twigs cracking beneath his massive paws as he hit the ground with a *thud*. He blew a breath through his nose, and she swallowed hard. *Uh oh.* His head was still down, his ears flat.

"Noah, it's me." Her hands trembled, so she clenched them into fists at her sides. "It's Amber."

He took a step toward her, and in his crouched position, he looked fierce. If she weren't alone in the woods with no way of knowing what was going on in his mind, she'd have been in awe. But Alexis's words rang in her mind: *you might end up his first meal.*

Slowly, carefully, she moved away, not daring to turn her back to him. Leaves crunched beneath her shoes, the sound melding with Noah's low growl like a warning. "Luke is on his way," she forced the whisper through her thickening throat.

He prowled toward her as she backed away. *Oh, shit.*

"Your alpha is coming." Gripping the side of the truck, she stepped on the tire and hauled herself into the bed.

Noah's growl intensified. Her pulse raced.

She lifted her hands, palms toward him, as he stalked around to the tailgate. *Come on, Luke. Where are you?* If she were a shifter herself, she could have sent her brother a mental message. Werewolves had a sort of telepathy in their wolf forms. Of course, if she were a shifter herself, she wouldn't be in this situation, about to become her best friend's dinner.

Noah rocked back on his haunches and sprang, landing in the bed of the truck, inches from Amber.

"Noah, no!" she screamed and scrambled onto the top of the cab. "I know you can understand me. Your wolf's instinct is to hunt, but the man should always be in control." How many times had she heard her father say those same words when he was alpha?

Noah knew the laws. He'd gone through training with Nylah when they were kids and everyone thought he'd be a shifter too. "Remember what you learned," she said as she scanned the branches above, calculating which one would hold her weight if she jumped. They were all too high to reach.

On her hands and knees, she inched backward before rolling onto the balls of her feet. As Noah rocked onto his haunches, preparing to lunge, her foot slipped, and she slid down the windshield onto the hood.

A howl echoed in the distance, and as she peered through the glass, she saw Noah's ears prick. He turned his head toward the sound and leaped from the bed of the truck onto the ground.

Amber rolled off the hood as quietly as she could and gently tugged on the door handle. The clicking of the door opening and the light from the cabin drew Noah's attention, and he spun around as she scrambled into the truck and slammed the door, hitting both locks and exhaling a curse.

Something was wrong. It was as if Noah didn't even recognize her. Like the man ceased to exist the moment the beast took over. Even the youngest, most inexperienced shifters had more control of their wolves.

Another howl sounded, unmistakably Luke, followed by several others, creating a symphony piercing enough to make even Amber's blood hum.

Noah turned toward the trees as a line of wolves approached the clearing. Luke stood in the middle, the biggest of the pack, with caramel-colored fur. Chase, his second in command with sleek black fur, flanked him on the right, and James stood to his left. Cade, Bryce, and Alexis made up the rest of the crew.

Luke held his head high and let out a commanding *woof*, followed by a low growl. Amber didn't need their special telepathy to understand the alpha was telling the fledgling to stand down. But Noah didn't follow orders. Instead, he stiffened, the fur on his back standing in a ridge, and he took a tentative step forward.

The alpha growled louder, moving toward him while the others fanned out in a semicircle, trapping Noah between the pack and the truck. Noah snarled and snapped, and the pack tightened the circle.

"What are you doing, Noah? You can't disobey the

alpha." Luke would be fully justified in tearing Noah apart if he continued this insolence.

A knock sounded on the glass behind her, and she squealed. She turned around to find Rain, an elemental witch and Chase's fate-bound, tugging on the door handle. Amber reached across the seat and popped the lock, and Rain slid inside.

"Chase asked me to come in case he was under a spell, but I guess he isn't." She tucked her dark, curly hair behind her ear and gave Amber a sympathetic look.

"With the way he's acting, I'm not so sure. He almost attacked me."

Her brow furrowed. "That doesn't sound right."

"I know. I was hoping Luke could calm him down, but he's acting like the man doesn't exist at all anymore." She turned her gaze back to the confrontation outside.

Luke and Noah stood nearly nose to nose, the alpha calm and stoic, while Noah bared his teeth. Luke didn't waver, and she could sense the dominant, patient vibes he exuded as he tried to get the wild wolf under control.

But Noah wasn't having it. He lunged, latching on to Luke's shoulder and trying to drag him to the ground. The other wolves closed in, and Amber held her breath, praying to every god in existence that her best friend would survive.

"He won't kill him, will he?" Rain asked.

"I hope not." Her brother was a kind, just alpha, but he was still alpha. One out-of-control wolf could wreak havoc on the pack structure.

Luke spun, throwing Noah to the ground, but he got back up and snarled some more. He lunged again, but this time, Luke caught him by the neck and sent him careening into a tree trunk. The wood cracked with the impact, and Noah hit the ground with a *thud*.

The wolves circled him again, and again he rose to his feet, letting out an enraged howl. He barreled toward Luke, and they rolled over each other, snapping and snarling like they were fighting to the death.

"Stop it." Amber's breath fogged the glass. "They have to stop." She unlocked the door and threw it open.

"Amber, no." Rain clutched her arm, but she pulled from her grasp, sliding out of the truck and running toward the fray.

"Stop it! Noah, stop. It's Luke. He's your alpha."

Noah jerked his head toward her and whined as Luke clamped onto his throat.

"Luke, it's Noah." She clasped her hands in front of her chest. "Please. Both of you."

Noah whined again, and Luke loosened his grip.

"Stand down," she pleaded. "Please take control. I can't lose you too."

Something sparked in Noah's eyes, and as Luke released his hold, he bowed his head, tucking his tail and letting out a submissive whimper. Luke stood over him, tail high, chest proud, and Noah licked his muzzle, accepting his place in the pack.

Amber's breath came out in a rush as the other wolves relaxed their stances. Noah was safe…for now.

She leaned against the truck, pressing her fingers to her temples. As much as she wanted to be sure he was okay, she didn't dare go to him. He was docile now, lying on his stomach while Luke and Chase stood on either side of him, but Amber's pulse hadn't yet slowed to a normal rate. She had no idea if he was willingly compliant or if he was merely trying to stay alive.

A smaller, sandy-colored wolf approached, and in a mist of shimmering light, Alexis shifted into her human form. She wore beige cargo pants with a black tank top, and her short blonde hair was tucked behind her ears. Rain climbed out of the truck to stand next to Amber.

"Is he okay?" Amber's hands trembled again, so she crossed her arms, tucking them against her sides.

Alexis sighed, shaking her head. "His wolf is wild. I've never seen anything like it, and I was rogue most of my life."

"Is there any way I can help?" Rain asked. "A calming potion, maybe?"

"We're going to take him hunting," Alexis said. "Hopefully once he's fed, we can help him shift and figure out what's going on. His thoughts aren't on the same wavelength as ours. He can't communicate in wolf form."

Amber nodded. "Will you bring him back here when you're done? I'll wait."

"Luke wants you to go home. He'll be by to get your story later."

"Thank you." Amber waved as Alexis returned to wolf form and bounded into the trees after the others.

"I'm sorry about Nylah." Rain rested a hand on her shoulder. "I never met her, but Chase said y'all were close."

"She was my best friend. Both of them were." Amber smiled sadly, and a wave of dizziness washed over her. She clutched the side of Noah's truck to steady herself as a sinking sensation formed in her stomach. Another premonition was coming on.

"Are you okay?" Rain asked.

"I feel like…" She pressed her lips together and shook her head. It was impossible. "I feel like Nylah's still alive."

Rain tilted her head. "I thought the only way for Noah to shift was if his older sibling died prematurely."

"That's the only way I'm aware of, but these feelings are never wrong."

"How…?"

"I have no idea, but I'm going to find out."

## CHAPTER TEN

Alrick gazed at the Thropynite lying in his palm. The she-wolf had constructed a wire cage, attaching it to a chain she'd worn carelessly around her neck like an ornament. Had she no idea of this tiny shard's worth? Of its power? At its simplest, it gave magical beings the ability to shapeshift…an ability no one but the gargoyles should have. In the hands of the powerful, it could be used to meld the souls of two beings. No one knew the true origin of the stone, but the Sect believed it had been around as long as the earth itself.

He fastened the clasp behind his neck, letting the stone rest against his chest and relishing the extra magic it fed into his veins.

"It's only a matter of time now, brothers." He lay a hand on each of the three other gargoyles' shoulders in turn, checking their auras for signs of life. But the small piece of stone he'd retrieved from the she-wolf wasn't enough to bring life to them all.

Alrick was one of the originals, the first of his kind to be created. Later, the Sect discovered they had more control over their abominations if they used the Thropynite to create them, but then forbade them from having contact with it until they deemed it necessary.

His brothers in arms came from the second batch of recruits, and he would need a much larger piece of stone to revive them. Like the one his witch destroyed when she left him.

He gazed at the she-wolf, now in human form, lying unconscious on the bed his traitorous witch used to occupy. Her superficial wounds had nearly healed by the time he brought her into his home, but the blow to the head he'd given her when she resisted had knocked her out for two days. Now, she stirred.

Her long auburn hair spilled out in a tangle around her head, and she had a sprinkling of freckles across her nose that reminded him so much of his witch, his heart ached to look at her. Perhaps she was nothing more than a witch herself and the stone had given her the ability to transform into a wolf. He would soon find out.

"What the hell?" She blinked her brown eyes open and pressed a hand to her temple, rising onto an elbow. Turning her head, she took in her surroundings, confusion contorting her delicate features. "Am I dead?"

He could see how she might think so. His pocket dimension rendered the world around them colorless, as if they stood in a bubble in the middle of a fog.

"You're alive…for now." His gravelly voice startled her, and as she took in his form, she scrambled to her feet.

"Grunch." She tilted her head, squinting at him.

He cringed at the derogatory name. "I'm a gargoyle, not a Grunch. That name was given to us by the humans…the very people we were supposed to protect." They considered him and his brothers a family of albino deformities, with their stone-gray skin, hunched postures, and demon-like faces, and they exiled them to the outskirts of town. In their homeland, the gargoyles could transform completely to their human forms, but the piece of Thropynite they'd brought with them to New Orleans didn't have enough power for full transformations, so they were frozen in this abhorrent in-between state.

She scoffed and shook her head. "Protect them from what? You eat their hearts."

They had to keep their demon sides fed to maintain their power, much like a werewolf was compelled to hunt in his wolf form despite what the man had eaten. "We sacrifice a few to shelter the masses."

"From magic." She crossed her arms.

"Magic is an abomination."

"What do you think made you?"

"You know nothing about me," he growled. He was tempted to end this conversation for good and absorb her knowledge the demonic way, but she could be of use to him alive. "I will not tolerate your insolence, witch. Now, tell me how you acquired the Thropynite."

"I'm not a witch." She called on her magic and transformed into a snarling wolf.

Alrick grunted. She was a she-wolf, after all. The magic he used to create this small dimension normally kept both supernaturals and humans away. They couldn't sense the pocket lying parallel with their world, but they'd acquire a feeling of foreboding unease if they ventured anywhere near it. Perhaps the Thropynite had guided her here.

The wolf rocked back, preparing to spring, and Alrick crossed his thick arms. Baring her teeth, she lunged, aiming directly for his neck, but she slammed into the invisible wall of her cell, bouncing off and hitting the floor with a *thunk*. She sprang to her feet and dove to the side, where she encountered yet another wall.

"You won't escape." He sank into a chair he'd brought in from the earthly realm. "Your prison is fortified by magic only I can unravel." His threat wasn't entirely true. His witch had finally broken the spell after decades of imprisonment, but this she-wolf didn't possess the ability to undo demon magic.

She growled before transforming into a woman. "Do you hear yourself? You're using the very thing you're trying to rid the world of. You're the abomination."

"Indeed I am, as are my brothers." He gestured to the other gargoyles frozen in stone. "We cannot fight our demon natures, but it was a sacrifice we willingly made."

"To protect the masses."

"Precisely. And once we purge all the magic from the world, we will end our lives for the greater good." He cradled the Thropynite in his palm. "Where did you get this?"

She crossed her arms and inclined her chin.

"You will tell me." He rose to his feet and loomed toward her, but she simply shook her head, unfazed by his threatening stance. A strange flutter rose from his gut, her lack of fear intriguing him.

"Maybe you're not aware," she said, "but werewolves hunt demons. That makes me the predator and you the prey."

He lowered his brow. "Yet you're the one in a cage."

"For now." She lifted one shoulder dismissively. "But not for long. We hunt in packs."

He was well aware of how werewolves hunted. The mangey mongrels were the reason he and his brothers fled Europe. It was the only way to survive. Werewolves were intelligent and fierce, and this she-wolf was no exception. Hollow threats would get him nowhere with her.

"My name is Alrick," he said.

She let out a cynical laugh. "I'd say it's nice to meet you, but you've locked me in a cage in another dimension, and once I'm free, I'll send you back to hell where you belong."

He grunted. "I'm familiar with your instinct to rid the world of demons. The cage is simply for your safety."

"My safety? I think you mean your own."

"On the contrary. If you attempted to attack me, I would crush your skull, absorb your knowledge, and devour your heart."

"I'd like to see you try."

Another flutter rose from his gut. "It would be the last thing you saw, she-wolf."

"Don't call me she-wolf."

"What would you prefer I call you?"

"I'd prefer you let me out of this cage so I can kill you."

He chuckled. "You're going to be here for a while, *she-wolf*. Unless you want to tell me where you found this shard of Thropynite so I can acquire more, you'd best get comfortable."

"Bite me."

"Don't tempt me." He returned to the chair. "I was engaged to a witch before the Sect recruited me."

"Poor her." She remained standing, her arms crossed, feet wide. He could almost see the gears turning in her mind as she planned her escape.

"I didn't always look like this."

"Your point?" She pressed her fingertips against the

invisible wall, giving it a hard shove before returning to her guarded stance.

"You remind me of her. She was beautiful, intelligent, cunning…*insolent* like you."

"Lucky me."

"I don't want to kill you." Not yet anyway. She was far too intriguing. "Tell me your name."

She pursed her lips, her eyes calculating as she drummed her fingers on her biceps. Her jaw clenched, and she rested her hands on her hips. "It's Nylah."

## CHAPTER ELEVEN

His wolf had been ravenous. The magic had been dormant inside him for twenty-nine years, and as it rose to the surface, it had one thought on its mind: to feed.

Noah had tried to take control. Seeing the fear in Amber's eyes as he prowled around her—the way she screamed when he lunged—had ripped into his soul like a thousand razorblades.

He almost killed her.

She was his best friend, the one woman he could see himself spending forever with, and his wolf had tried to eat her. *Fuck.*

Now he sat in the passenger seat of Luke's truck, staring out the window into the swamp while his pack stood a few yards away and discussed what to do about his behavior.

*His* behavior. More like the behavior of a wild animal who had taken over his body. It wasn't supposed to be like this. He remembered Nylah's first shift as if it happened yesterday. They'd gone to the hunting grounds with their father and the alpha on the full moon after their thirteenth birthdays. When Nylah shifted and he didn't, she didn't try to attack. She'd obeyed the alpha like she would have in human form.

Even Bryce, a human who'd become a werewolf after being attacked and left for dead, had no problem obeying the alpha after his first shift.

So what the hell was Noah's problem?

Luke said something, though their voices were too quiet for him to hear, and Alexis lifted her arms, dropping them at her sides like she couldn't answer his question. Bryce shook his head and fisted his hand over his heart as he spoke. Chase said something, and Luke nodded before heading toward the truck.

Noah stared straight ahead as he climbed in and slammed the door. Thank the gods his wolf had finally submitted to the alpha. Now the best course of action for the man was not to speak until spoken to.

Luke kneaded the steering wheel, the tendons in his neck tight as he clenched his jaw. "First, I'm sorry about Nylah. I know you're grieving."

"Thank you." He lowered his head. He *should* have been grieving, but he and his twin shared a bond, what Cade called his Wonder Twin senses. Somewhere, deep inside his soul, the bond was still there, unbroken.

It didn't make sense. The only way he could have inherited the shifting ability was if Nylah died...yet he couldn't ignore his gut instinct that she was still alive.

"What the hell happened out there?" Luke started the engine and pulled out onto the road.

"I'd say I lost control of my wolf, but I never had it to begin with. The moment I shifted, the animal took over."

Luke glanced at him before focusing on the road. "You could have killed her."

"I know. I'm sorry." Sorry didn't begin to describe his level of regret. "Are you going to see her now?"

"I am."

"Can I come? I want to apologize."

Luke sighed and gave him a curt nod. "You can. Maybe hearing her side of the story will help you gain some control. I've never seen her so terrified."

His throat thickened. Neither had he.

"Until you do gain control, you will not shift without me present. Do you understand?"

"Yes."

"Tomorrow night, and every other night until I deem it unnecessary, you will hunt with me. Clear your calendar."

"Okay." Noah fought the urge to sink in his seat. It was bad enough being babysat while he was on probation, but this was humiliating. Though, after the way his new wolf had behaved, he understood. He deserved worse.

"And no more patrols until you have control of your wolf. I want you indoors by nightfall unless you're with me."

"Understood." He was a grown-ass man being put back on the leash…a disgrace to his pack.

Luke parked behind Amber's Mazda in her driveway and killed the engine. Noah slid out of the truck and followed him to the door. When Amber answered, her eyes tightened as she met his gaze, driving a knife into his heart.

How could he have done that to her? His wolf should have claimed her as his fate-bound the moment he emerged, not tried to make a meal out of her.

She stepped aside and motioned for them to enter, so he followed Luke into the living room. As Amber joined them, Noah took her hand in both of his. "I'm so sorry."

"I know." She gave him a tight-lipped smile and tugged from his grasp, twisting the knife even deeper.

"Can I get you guys a beer?" she asked. "After tonight, we could all use one."

Noah waited for Luke to answer "yes" before nodding and saying, "Thanks."

As Amber disappeared into the kitchen, Noah sank onto the sofa and Luke took the teal accent chair adjacent to it. A fireplace with a white brick mantel occupied the wall across from him, and he caught his reflection in the blank screen of the television mounted above it. His hair was disheveled, so he ran a hand through it and cast his gaze to the potted ivy in the window instead. He couldn't bear to look at himself.

Amber returned with three bottles of Blue Moon and sat on the corner of the couch, as far away from Noah as she could get.

"Walk me through it from the beginning," Luke said.

Noah took a long drink from his beer, focusing on the way the citrusy bubbles cooled his throat as Amber recounted the incident step by step.

"I'm glad you got there when you did," she said. "I don't know what would have happened otherwise."

"You have to know that wasn't me." Noah scooted toward her and pleaded with his eyes. "I was there, like a floating subconscious, but I had zero control over what the wolf did. It didn't know who you are. It didn't know how important you are to me."

She looked into his eyes, her voice thin. "You scared me."

"I'm sorry." He scooted closer until his knee touched hers. "You helped me. When you got out of the truck and yelled at us, that was what brought me to the surface and let me take control. I don't know what would have happened if you weren't there." *She wouldn't have been in danger if she wasn't, dumbass.*

"Somebody had to talk some sense into you." She gave him a small smile. "Don't let it happen again."

"I won't."

"He'll be under close observation," Luke said.

*Like a puppy on a leash.* Noah set his beer on the coffee table. Amber took another drink from hers, and when she reached toward the table to place hers next to his, it slipped from her grasp.

Noah instinctively stretched his mind, using the energy in the air to grip the bottle before it could spill. With a flick of his wrist, he positioned it upright on the table. Amber didn't flinch at his use of power; he'd been doing things like that around her for as long as he could remember.

Luke cocked his head. "Interesting. Your wolf was out of control, but your second-born gift seems unaffected by the change."

"Why would it be affected?"

"Most lose their gift when their dormant wolf is awakened. It's rare for a shifter to have any other abilities, unless they have witch or Voodoo ancestry."

"Lucky me." He'd gladly give up his telekinesis if it would tame the rabid beast inside him. Even now, sitting in Amber's living room, his wolf was restless. Though he lacked the connection to understand and communicate with it, he could tell it wanted to run…to hunt…and it took every ounce of willpower he could muster to keep the animal subdued.

"Are you okay?" Amber's eyes held concern…and a hint of fear. "You look pale."

He glanced at the alpha. "The moon is calling me, I guess. My wolf wants to hunt again."

"The pull is always strongest on a full moon. Tomorrow it should be easier to control. You'll sleep in our spare bedroom tonight in case anything happens."

Noah held in his groan. He wasn't just being babysat. Now he had to have a slumber party too.

"Do you want to inform your parents about Nylah, or should I?" Luke asked.

He clenched his teeth. He didn't want anyone to tell them anything. Not while he felt his sister could still be out there. "I will."

"No." Amber shook her head. "Nylah isn't dead."

Luke straightened, looking at her quizzically. "Details?"

"You know by now details are scarce. She's out there somewhere, and she needs us to find her."

Luke rubbed his thumb and forefinger on his chin. "Not to discredit your ability, but is it possible your desire for her to be alive is clouding your senses?"

"I don't think so."

"She's right," Noah said. "I can feel it too. If she were dead, I'd know."

Luke stood and paced into the kitchen to toss his bottle in the recycle bin. Noah looked at Amber, and she mouthed the words, "Thank you."

"If she is alive, how do you explain your new ability to shift?" Luke stood behind the chair, resting his hands on the back.

Noah took a deep breath and blew it out hard. He'd have to choose his words carefully, or he could end up incriminating both himself and his sister. "I think it could be the Thropynite. It has the power to grant shapeshifting abilities, and it can be used to fuse two souls into one body."

Amber gasped. "That makes sense."

Luke sank into the chair and rested his elbows on his knees. "How do you know so much about the stone?"

Noah grabbed his beer and took a long drink, hoping to wash down the knot in his throat. It didn't help. "When you mentioned it the other day, I did some research online. A stone that could awaken my wolf sounded too good to be true, so I was curious." That was only a half-lie. Both he and Nylah had researched the Thropynite extensively, long before she left the pack.

Luke arched a brow. "Do you have the stone?"

"No, of course not." He didn't, but Nylah most likely did.

"The Thropynite must be in New Orleans, and it awakened your wolf along with the Grunch." Amber rested her hand on top of his, and his chest tightened.

Luke lowered his brow. "If that were the case, every second-born in the area would be a shifter now."

"But Noah was supposed to be one," Amber said. "He's a twin…the only one in our pack."

Luke studied him, narrowing his eyes as if processing the idea. "I'll put another call in to the congress tomorrow. We don't have enough information on the Thropynite to confirm your theory. I don't trust the internet; people can post anything there." He rose to his feet and looked at his sister. "Are you okay?"

"I'm fine." She released Noah's hand and stood.

"Let's head home." Luke strode toward the door. "We can swing by your place to pick up some clothes."

"Okay." Noah rose and followed him to the door.

"Do you mind if I talk to Noah alone for a minute?" Amber asked.

"I'll be in the truck." Luke gave his sister a quick hug and strode out the door.

Amber chewed her bottom lip as her brother walked away, and she turned to Noah. "We didn't get to finish our conversation, and I know now isn't the time. Do you want to have dinner tomorrow night? I get off at eight."

"I have to hunt with Luke tomorrow night."

"Oh, okay." Disappointment was evident in her eyes.

He knew where the conversation would lead. He had a wolf now, so he didn't have an excuse for not being with her. Hell, he *wanted* to be with her. "I'm free the next night."

She smiled. "It's a date."

He turned to leave, but she caught him by the hand. "Is there something you're not telling me about Nylah?"

He forced his gaze to her eyes and shook his head. "I'll see you the day after tomorrow." He kissed her cheek and strode out the door.

# CHAPTER TWELVE

Amber sat in her office, her desk in perpetual disarray, and went over the bar's inventory orders for the week. They were running dangerously low on hurricane mix, so she'd have to pay extra for rush shipping. The syrupy-sweet rum drinks were a top seller, thanks to the buy-one-get-one-free special they ran for tourists who signed up for the haunted history tours that operated out of a side room in the bar.

Every evening at six and eight, the place would be packed with visitors taking them up on their special drink offer. Half an hour later, things would be quiet again.

She glanced at the clock on her computer. Five-thirty. It was time to help Kaci get ready for the rush.

A few tourists had already wandered into the bar, their blue wristbands indicating they'd leave with the first tour group. Kaci had set up a row of black plastic cups across one side of the bar and was filling them with ice as Amber lifted the hinged section of the counter and joined her. A cylindrical cooler filled with premixed hurricanes sat to her right, and she grabbed a few cups, filling them with the red liquid.

As she set them on the bar, her head spun, and an overwhelming feeling about her employee seeped into her soul. "Kaci, are you mated?"

She laughed. "Not hardly. I'm not even dating anyone."

Amber nodded. "You're about to be soon."

"Really?" Her eyes sparkled. "Is it Cade? God, I hope it's Cade."

"I didn't know you liked him."

"Who doesn't? He's the hottest shifter in the pack."

*Not anymore.* In Amber's eyes, Noah held that title now. "I don't feel like it's Cade, but that doesn't mean it can't be. Keep your mind open, though."

Within minutes, people packed the bar, filling every seat and most of the floor as they waited for their tours to begin. She and Kaci served drink after drink, ran credit cards, and made change until the final tourist strolled out the front door.

"Whew!" Kaci wiped the counter with a dishrag. "Those tours are getting more and more popular."

"They won a few awards this year, so they're getting a lot of free promotion." Amber pulled bottles of light and dark rum from a cabinet and began mixing the drinks for the next rush when a man with long brown hair and a stocky build strode through the door.

"Welcome to O'Malley's." Kaci beamed a smile as he approached, and his gaze locked on her.

"Amber?" He stopped at the bar and rested his hands on the surface.

"That's me." Amber brushed her hair from her face and moved toward him. "How can I help you?"

The guy looked like it pained him to tear his gaze away from Kaci to look at her. "Hi." He glanced at Kaci again before continuing. "I'm Judd Wilson. Your father contacted me and suggested I stop by to say 'hello.'"

*Not again.* She really needed to have a conversation with her dad. Now he was sending them in unannounced. What was next? A guy showing up in a tux with a ring in his hand? "It's nice to meet you, Judd, but I'm afraid you've been sent here under false pretenses. I'm not in the market for a mate."

"I see." He couldn't seem to stop his gaze from flicking to Kaci.

"I hope you didn't drive far." Amber lifted the flap in the counter, ready to escape to the back room. She didn't need any kind of empathic ability to see what was happening between Judd and Kaci. This was a fate-bound bond forming.

"I came in from Lake Charles."

"Well, you're welcome to stay and have a drink or two on the house. Kaci will take care of you." She winked at her bartender and slipped into her office.

*Damn.* She didn't realize Kaci would find her mate *that* soon. And at only twenty-two years old. She was a lucky girl.

Two hours later, when Amber returned to the bar for the second rush, Judd was still there, making heart eyes at Kaci as she prepared the drinks. The man exuded love. There was no doubt in Amber's mind Kaci was his fate-bound, and seeing the joy it brought him…knowing the happiness he'd feel for the rest of his life…Amber's resolve to not mate with a shifter unless his wolf claimed her solidified.

So what did that mean for her and Noah?

After the rush, Kaci began to wipe down the bar, but Amber took the rag. "Why don't you take off early? I'll close up tonight."

Kaci bit her bottom lip and glanced at Judd. "Are you sure?"

"Absolutely." She leaned toward her and whispered, "I'm happy for you."

When Kaci left, Amber retrieved her laptop from her office and sat at the bar. It was a weeknight, and no festivals were going on, so the rest of the evening would be slow. She occupied herself with work to keep her mind off her current predicament, but she couldn't stop her thoughts from wandering to Noah. Even with closing time approaching, she remained at the bar, pondering what to do.

"Hey, Amber. You're working late tonight." Odette sashayed through the front door, carrying a big cardboard box. Her curly black hair spiraled down to her shoulders, and she wore her signature colors, purple and black, to honor Baron Samedi, the Voodoo spirit who guided her.

Amber closed her laptop and lifted a half-empty mug of beer. "Not really working. I wasn't ready to go home." Truth be told, she was hoping Noah and the hunting party would stop by for a drink when they were done. "What do you have for me? That looks like more than I ordered."

Odette slid the box onto the bar and took the seat next to Amber. "I brought you some swag to give to your customers." She pulled out a stack of coasters and a small cardboard box. Tape sealed the edges, so Amber tugged her trusty Swiss Army knife from her pocket and sliced it open to find shot glasses with the distillery's logo, a skeleton wearing a top hat, painted on them. Odette was

James's mate, and she ran the popular rum company, The Baron.

"Thanks. These are great." Amber wiped the condensation off the side of her glass.

"James told me about what happened with Noah. How are you holding up?"

"I'm fine. I just… I didn't expect…" She didn't expect to nearly be eaten by the magical beast who was supposed to make Noah fall instantly in love with her. "When you met James, how long did it take before his wolf claimed you? Was it immediate?"

Odette returned the swag items to the box and pushed it away before swiveling on her stool to face Amber. "That was a special circumstance, what with the reincarnation business and all. It took him a while to sort it all out."

Amber sipped her beer. "Once he did figure it out, when he knew you were his fate-bound, did you feel it too?" She'd never thought to ask a shifter's mate what it felt like to be claimed. Based on the way Luke and the others talked about it, and how giddy Kaci was with Judd, she assumed the feeling worked both ways. But after the way Noah's wolf terrified her, she couldn't imagine feeling any kind of connection to the beast, no matter how desperately she wanted to.

"I knew he was the one before he did, but again, that was due to our circumstances." She smiled knowingly. Through her Voodoo priestess, Odette had done a series of past-life regressions, so she knew she'd been with James in previous lifetimes. "I don't think it feels the same as it does for a shifter. You and I don't have a second soul to guide us like they do, but I do sense a connection like no other. It feels as if a cord runs from my core to his, tethering us. An unbreakable bond. But I'm a Vodouisant, and you're a werewolf. It might be completely different for you."

"Hmm." She drained the rest of her beer. Aside from being terrified of Noah's wolf, her feelings for him hadn't changed since he shifted. The connection she felt to him was simply a woman falling in love with her best friend.

Odette placed her hand on top of Amber's. "Give it time. Your case is unique as well. Most shifters have known their wolves for ten or fifteen years before they claim a mate. Noah only met his yesterday."

"You're right. I shouldn't have expected him to claim me the moment he came into existence. He's not a baby duck. I have to be patient."

"Your ability doesn't give a glimpse into how it might work out?"

She laughed. "Sadly, I've never had a premonition about myself. And Noah…" She shook her head. "I sensed change coming for him, but my emotions get in the way when it comes to him. I should have warned him."

"I'm sure you did what you thought was right." She slipped her purse strap onto her shoulder. "Even if his wolf doesn't claim you, y'all have a lifetime of friendship behind you. That's the best foundation for a relationship I can imagine."

Amber shook her head. "I could never do that to him. If he doesn't claim me, I'll have to end it." And then she might have to take her mother up on her offer of having that party. She shuddered at the thought of being put on display for other packs, but it would be better than the random ambushes her dad was planning.

Odette stood. "If you want to stop by the temple sometime, we can leave an offering for Erzulie, the loa of love. She might help you." Loa were Voodoo spirits. They weren't gods, but they did have the power to help people in situations like this.

"Thanks. I'll think about it." She slid off her stool, preparing to take the box to the storage closet when her head spun for the second time that evening. She pressed the heel of her hand to her temple as the familiar sinking sensation brought on another empathic premonition. "Whoa."

"Are you okay?" Odette placed a hand on her shoulder.

"There's going to be another murder."

---

Noah ran beside Luke, twigs crunching beneath his paws as his wolf pushed his body to its limits. He'd shifted easily, his beast coming to the surface on command as if he'd been there his entire life. Following commands from the alpha was another story.

Luke stopped abruptly, his ears pricking as he gazed at a pair of gators lying in the mud near the water's edge. Noah started toward them, his wolf eager for a fight, but a growl from the alpha signaled he should wait. They'd already hunted. He'd satiated his hunger, but electricity hummed through his veins, the urge to engage with the potential prey overwhelming him.

Crouching, he began his advance, and Luke's growl turned into a snarl. The alpha had issued an order, and Noah had to obey. He fought for control, wrestling with the wolf in his mind, but the beast refused to listen. He continued his pursuit.

Luke leaped in front of him, blocking his path and snapping at his face. The alpha's teeth grazed his muzzle, and Noah growled against his will. Luke growled in return, exerting his dominance until finally, Noah's wolf surrendered. With a whine, he lay on his belly and watched as the gators disappeared into the murky water. Luke shifted, and Noah tried to follow suit, but his wolf wouldn't release control.

"Return to human form," Luke commanded.

Noah clawed his way to the surface and was finally able to shift. Hanging his head, he stood before his alpha. "I'm sorry. I swear it's not me disobeying you. I don't know why my wolf won't listen."

Luke walked up the path toward his truck, and Noah followed. "You still can't sense my thoughts? No form of telepathy at all?"

"None. I'm going off body language and instinct." He climbed into the passenger seat and slammed the door. What the hell was wrong with him? All he'd wanted his entire life was to be a shifter, and now that he had a wolf, the damn beast was out of control.

"I've never heard of anything like this." Luke started the engine and pulled out onto the road. "But that doesn't mean it's never happened. I'll call the congress to see if a case like this is on record somewhere."

Noah grunted. "Can we wait a week or two and see if it fixes itself? I don't want the entire werewolf population knowing what a screwup I am." It was bad enough when he was a rare twin who couldn't shift. He didn't need the added humiliation.

Luke shook his head. "If this goes downhill, it's my responsibility as alpha. Issues like this are required to be reported. I'll contact my father. He'll be discreet."

"Thanks, man." Noah rubbed his forehead, cursing

himself silently. He had to get his wolf under control, not just for himself, but for his pack.

Luke's phone rang from his pocket, and he dug it out before pressing it to his ear. "Yeah." His jaw clenched, his fingers curling around the steering wheel in a death grip. "Where?" He blew out a hard breath. "I'm on my way."

He dropped his phone into the cupholder. "That was Cade. There's been another one. A Vodouisant this time. Heart ripped out like the others. Can I count on you to keep control?"

Could he? Not really. No. "You know I'll do my best."

Luke nodded, but his expression was grim. They parked in front of a bar on the outskirts of the city, and he killed the engine. "We can't chance your wolf going rogue during a fight."

"Understood." Noah climbed out of the truck and followed the alpha into the woods behind the bar.

Cade met them beneath a massive oak tree a few yards away. "It's back here. The beast had the decency to drag his victim away from prying eyes this time, but it won't be long until the smell draws attention."

"He's getting smarter," Luke grumbled as they made their way toward the body.

The previous corpses had been discovered right in the middle of the French Quarter. No one had witnessed the actual crimes, but the gargoyle-like demon Noah and Cade had found in the cemetery had to be responsible.

James and Chase stood over the victim, and Chase gestured to the chest wound as they approached. "Looks like claws, same as the others, but check this out." He moved to stand at what was left of the woman's head.

Noah exhaled sharply as he took in the carnage. The skull

had been pierced in multiple places, as if by claws, and the eyes bulged from their sockets. "Are we sure the same creature did this? The woman I found last month didn't have this kind of head wound, nor did the werewolf we found in the street."

"The second victim did," Luke said. "Do you know if the police have been contacted?"

"Not yet. I believe we're the only ones who know," James said. "I called Odette. She's on her way to identify the body."

"What brought you out here?" Luke moved around the body, examining it. "This isn't the normal patrol area."

"Amber called," Cade said. "She sensed something was going down in the area, so we came out to have a look."

"The wounds look fresh," Chase said. "I'd say this happened less than an hour ago."

Noah ground his teeth, a strange sensation of jealousy churning in his gut. It was ridiculous, but he couldn't help wondering why she chose to notify Cade over him. He'd never been jealous before. Could this be his wolf beginning to claim her? He could only hope.

"When she couldn't get ahold of you," Cade said to Luke, "she went down the chain until she reached one of us."

The tightness in Noah's chest eased. As a former non-shifter, he didn't have a place on the call chain. Of course she wouldn't contact him about this. It was pack business, not personal.

"Do you think we're dealing with the Grunch?" James asked.

"I'm not positive," Luke said. "But based on the information we've gathered, I assume so."

Noah gazed at the mangled body lying in the dirt. If Nylah really did find the Thropynite, the creature might have gone after her first. His connection to his sister and Amber's insistence that she was still alive were the only things keeping him from fearing she'd met the same fate.

The sound of a branch breaking drew their attention to the east, and Luke held up a hand indicating they should wait as he crept toward it. Shuffling sounded, and the bushes rustled like something was attempting to escape.

"Shit. Let's go." Luke transformed into his wolf, and the others followed suit, darting into the trees.

Noah stood there squeezing his fists, fighting the urge to shift, Luke's words echoing in his mind: *We can't chance your wolf going rogue during a fight.* He took a deep breath to steady himself and ran into the woods behind them. But as he approached and found his pack encircling the same stone-like creature he'd encountered before, he couldn't simply stand aside and watch. He had to help, so he shifted and joined the other wolves.

The creature smelled like a demon, of rotten garbage and sulfur, but it lacked the signature red eyes that most possessed. Its skin was gray and cracked, and blood stained its crooked mouth. Not mildew like he'd originally thought.

Luke lunged, snapping his jaws at the creature's flesh, but the demon was too fast. It teleported, shooting deeper into the woods.

The alpha grunted, and the others bobbed their heads as if they had received a message. But Noah's wild wolf heard nothing. He'd be of no use to them if he couldn't follow orders, and he didn't know the plan without the telepathic bond he should have shared with his packmates.

The wolves fanned out around the creature, lunging

and snapping, but the beast bounced from position to position, always out of their grasp.

Noah reached out with his senses, trying to manipulate the energy around him, but in his wolf form it seemed he couldn't access his telekinetic ability.

*Come on, buddy*, he said to his wolf in his mind. *Give me back control.*

He struggled, his wolf battling him for dominance. The beast did not want to let go. The fight continued in front of him, but he focused inward, willing his human side to come to the surface. His wolf snarled then let out a pained yelp. Cade swung his head around to look at Noah, and the demon used the distraction to his advantage, swiping his massive claws into Cade's shoulder and knocking him into a tree.

*Fuck.* He shouldn't have shifted. In this form, he was nothing more than a hindrance. Cade scrambled to his feet and limped away from the fight to heal, while Noah forced his wolf to grit his teeth, biting until he tasted blood. His body hummed, and though his wolf dug in his claws, trying with all his might to hold on, Noah beat him down and shifted to his human form.

Holding out his arms, he gathered the energy around him, sending out an invisible wave of force and freezing the massive demon to its spot. Luke attacked, sinking his teeth into its side, and Noah released the fiend, allowing the alpha to drag it to the ground.

The other wolves sprang, a mass of fur and fangs covering the creature as they snarled and growled, but a menacing laugh reverberated through the forest.

They froze, silent. Chase backed up, and Noah moved to the side to get a view of the demon, but it was gone.

Cade, now healed, took off with James to scout the area, but the gargoyle-demon had vanished.

As the men shifted back into their human forms, Luke looked at Noah. "You held him with your ability?"

Noah nodded. "I never should have shifted, but when I saw all of you on the move, I couldn't help myself. I'm sorry." He lowered his head, preparing for his punishment.

"That's understandable," Cade said. "Remember what it was like when we were kids? If we were around our parents when they shifted, we couldn't resist."

Noah inclined his chin toward Cade, silently thanking his friend for sticking up for him.

"You're right," Luke agreed. "I shouldn't expect him to have any more control than a young wolf would."

Noah's ears burned. The alpha may not expect him to have more control, but *he* expected himself to. He'd never be allowed to patrol with the pack if he didn't get his shit together, and he *definitely* couldn't be Amber's potential mate in this condition. They wouldn't allow his defective wolf to taint the alpha line.

# CHAPTER THIRTEEN

"Is this your alpha?" Alrick shoved the tuft of fur he'd ripped from the wolf's hide through the magical prison wall.

Nylah's jaw clenched as she leaned toward his hand, and her nostrils flared, her pupils constricting as the scent registered. He sensed the flush of heat running through her veins, and while her skin didn't turn to gooseflesh, the fine hairs on her arms rose on end. Just as he suspected. The local werewolf pack—*her* pack—had noticed his presence. She would pay for their attack.

"What did you do to him?" The she-wolf moved to snatch the token, but he grabbed her wrist with his other hand.

He jerked her forward, slamming her head into the prison wall and bloodying her nose. The vexatious woman minimized her reaction, so he yanked again, releasing her when her nose broke with a satisfying *pop*.

"Son of a bitch!" She backed away, out of his reach, and clutched her face. Deep purple spread outward beneath her eyes, and she winced as she pushed the bone back into place.

Tough girl. Her abominable magic would heal her far too quickly. He dropped the wolf fur into her prison, and she scrambled to grab it. The blood had already ceased its flow from her nostrils. *Infuriating.*

"Did you hurt him?" Her voice held far more accusation than a woman in her position should dare.

"I did nothing to him, but he did this to me." He gestured to his shoulder, where the biggest wolf's teeth had penetrated his skin, cutting all the way to the bone. The extra piece of Thropynite he'd taken from Nylah had made him both stronger and more vulnerable at the same time. His flesh, which formerly had the strength of stone, had softened, turning to the consistency of skin in some places.

"Next time he'll do worse." She set the fur on the small table inside her cell, the same table where his witch would keep the flowers he brought to brighten her mood.

Alrick's chest ached at the unwelcome memory, and he rotated his shoulder to try and ease the pain. His skin was slowly mending itself, but he'd need to feed a few more times to regain his strength.

"Doubtful. There were four wolves, and they couldn't lay a claw on me. If it weren't for the man who accompanied them, with his blasphemous powers, I could have taunted them until they passed out from exhaustion."

"What man?" Her eyes narrowed, her fingers curling at her sides.

*Interesting.* He tilted his head. "He was some sort of witch with powers I've rarely encountered before. He held me still with his mind, which allowed the wolves to attack."

She rushed toward him, slamming into the invisible cell wall and rubbing her forehead. When she recovered, she pressed her palms against the barrier. "He's no witch. He's my brother, and if you lay a finger on him, I swear to God, I'll tear you into so many pieces, no one will even know you existed."

Alrick was fiercely protective of someone once, and look where that got him. "Perhaps when I tire of our conversations, I'll let you try. If you continue to take the Lord's name in vain, I'll be the one doing the shredding."

She scoffed. "Do you hear yourself? You were made from a fucking demon, yet you claim to be doing the work of God."

His jaw clenched. "Because I sacrificed myself for the greater good."

"Yeah. Keep telling yourself that."

He turned a chair around backward, straddling it and resting his arms on the back. "Tell me about your brother."

"No."

"Tell me where you found the Thropynite."

"Go fuck yourself."

She was feisty, much like his witch. Nylah's resemblance to her may have been the only thing stopping him from digging his claws into her skull and retrieving all the information at once.

"You love him. I can see that." When she didn't respond, he continued, "I once cared for someone enough to risk my life to protect her." A mistake which added fuel to the demonic rage inside him.

"Your fiancée?" She sat in the chair next to the small table, arching a brow in defiance.

"She was one of the forsaken, like yourself. A witch." He chuckled, though he wasn't sure why. Simply talking about the treacherous woman tore his heart to shreds. "I loved her in spite of her ungodly magic."

"How very kind of you."

"When the Sect recruited me, I was forced to cut ties with her, but my love for her never ceased. We were to raid her village, killing all the forsaken in a single night, but I couldn't allow her to be harmed. I warned her. I bought her passage on a ship to New Orleans and begged her to start a new life, out of the Sect's reach."

"Let me guess. You missed her so much, you followed her here to live happily ever after."

"I missed her, yes, but there is no happily ever after in store for me. She followed my instructions and fled to America, while I stayed in Europe and thinned out the supernatural population."

She crossed her arms. "And what brought you to my lovely town? Your Sect trying to expand its reach? Are there others like you here?"

"We are the only ones, to my knowledge." He gestured to his brothers. "As for what brought us here, it was your kind. The werewolves of Paris organized all the neighboring packs into an army. They were the only ones who could sense our true nature in our human forms, so they attacked us when we were at our weakest, murdering us in masses. The Sect disbanded our legion, abandoning us, so I and my brothers fled to save our souls."

"Your true nature is hard to miss. Have you looked in a mirror lately?"

"We brought a piece of the Thropynite with us, for without it, we turn to stone ourselves." He cast his gaze to his brothers. "But it wasn't enough. We lost the ability to shift from human to gargoyle, getting stuck in this halfway rendering of both our forms."

"And I guess your witch took one look at you and told you to fuck off."

A growl rumbled in his chest. "She would not have me, but I could not live without her. I brought her here to the room you now reside in. Time moves at a crawl in this dimension, so she was mine for one hundred years."

"Then you got tired of her and killed her?"

He should have. "She tricked me and escaped. She destroyed the Thropynite, turning us to stone, and we've been frozen ever since…until you brought a piece here. Where did you find it?"

She pursed her lips and narrowed her eyes, refusing to speak.

"I'll need to feed again to heal this wound. Your brother's magic is formidable. I love the taste of a powerful heart."

Her eyes widened. "You wouldn't."

He laughed. "You know what I am and my purpose in life. What reason would make you doubt my word?"

"Kill me. Take my heart."

"Oh, but I enjoy your company far too much. You'll either tell me what I want to know, or your brother will be my next meal."

## CHAPTER FOURTEEN

"You didn't have to cook." Noah sat at the table in Amber's kitchen while she finished making dinner. "We could have ordered takeout."

She set a plate of crawfish étouffée in front of him and took the seat beside him. "I don't mind. I actually enjoy cooking, and it's not every day I have someone else to cook for." She gazed into his eyes, staring longer than comfortable, willing the connection between them to form. Surely if his wolf had claimed her, he would have said something. She'd made her interest in him clear, so there was no chance of him scaring her away.

She didn't feel the tether that Odette described magically forming, so she looked away and shrugged. "Besides, with the curfew Luke put on the pack, it's obviously not safe to be out in the Quarter at night. I couldn't endanger the life of a delivery person."

"Good point." He took a bite of his dinner. "This is delicious."

"Thanks. It's my mom's recipe."

They ate in silence for a while because she couldn't

make herself bring up the conversation they'd left unfinished a few nights ago. Honestly, she hoped he would bring it up, but he seemed content to eat his meal, smiling at her occasionally as if the kiss they shared never happened.

"Any news on Nylah?" she asked.

He swallowed his food, his eyes growing wide briefly before he spoke, "The pack is searching the area around Grunch Road and where we found the body for any signs that she might…for signs of her. So far, they've found nothing. Any news on your end?"

She shook her head. "I still feel like she's alive, but that's all I'm getting."

"Me too."

Amber chewed the inside of her cheek. She'd known Noah all her life, and the tension in his shoulders combined with the way his gaze darted about the room made it obvious he was holding something back.

"Luke said you helped them with the Grunch last night." Between running the bar and being the alpha's sister, Amber was privy to more information than a normal pack member would be. Plus, she drilled her brother with questions this morning when she found out Noah had been on the scene with him.

"I don't know how much I helped. The bastard still got away."

"Yeah, but they never would have come close to catching him if not for you. I guess you're getting more control over your wolf?"

"I don't know about that either." He shoved another scoop of étouffée into his mouth, avoiding eye contact.

"You'll get there, I'm sure." She reached across the table and placed her hand on top of his.

His breath caught at the contact, and he looked at their joined hands before gazing into her eyes. "I have no control. I shouldn't have shifted last night when the others took off to fight the Grunch. Cade was injured because of me."

"That's normal." She laced her fingers through his. "With the moon nearly full, and your packmates shifting, how could you resist? Even Luke was like that when his wolf first awoke."

Noah shook his head. "I'm not thirteen. It feels like I've got an alien living inside my body, battling me for dominance. I'm out of control."

She traced her thumb over his. "I'm not afraid of you."

"You should be." He slipped from her grasp, resting his hand in his lap.

Amber picked up her fork and pushed the food around on her plate. "Your wolf knows me now. That won't happen again."

"You don't know that."

"Yes, I do. I have powers too, remember?" Honestly, she *didn't* know. She'd had no more premonitions about Noah since she'd sensed his change, but logic told her she was right. His wolf didn't know who she was then; now it did. Problem solved.

She watched him eat for a few more minutes. Ever since she'd mentioned his sister, his demeanor had changed. He seemed nervous now, as if he had a secret. "What are you not telling me about Nylah?"

He froze with the fork halfway to his mouth before looking at her and returning it to his plate. "Nothing."

"You're lying." She leaned her forearms on the table, holding his gaze. "You can trust me."

Sighing, he lowered his head and tugged a slip of

paper from his pocket. He held it tightly, the tip of his thumb turning white from the pressure before he handed it to her. She unfolded it and read the words on the page.

*I can't tell you where I'm going or why, but I promise to return with an answer to your prayers.*

"This is Nylah's handwriting. When did she give you this?"

"She put it on my dresser the night she left."

She turned the page over, looking for more information, but the single sentence was all she'd written. "You knew she didn't go rogue?"

"No, I had no idea she left to work for the congress. This is all she told me."

She read the words again, realization dawning. "'An answer to your prayers.' Do you think Nylah brought the Thropynite here?"

"I know she did. Look." He showed her a series of texts he'd received.

"These are all from different numbers."

"Burner phones. I've tried replying, but the messages don't go through. My prayer was to awaken my wolf, and Nylah answered it."

"And woke the Grunch in the process. Holy crap." She gave the note back to him, and he folded it before returning it to his pocket. "This is bad, Noah. If Luke finds out…" She shook her head. "If the *congress* finds out she was the cause of the very thing she was sent to investigate…"

"I know. We'll both be dogfood. That's why you can't tell anyone about this. How the stone got here doesn't matter. The pack just needs to find Nylah and stop the Grunch."

She nodded. "You're absolutely right. We'll keep it

between us. I'm sure she had no idea bringing the Thropynite here would awaken the Grunch." How could she? Information on the stone was so scarce, it was thought to be merely a legend until now.

"Thank you." He took her hand beneath the table, and his magic vibrated across her skin, stronger than it had ever been.

"What are friends for?" She laced her fingers through his, sandwiching his hand between both of hers. "Thank *you* for trusting me."

As she held his gaze, something passed between them, like the shared secret formed a bond, deepening their relationship. He smiled and brushed a strand of hair from her forehead before gliding his fingers down her cheek in a much more intimate way than a friend would touch her.

Rising, she carried their empty plates to the sink, grabbed two more beers from the fridge, and padded toward the living room. Noah followed and sank onto the sofa next to her. He took a drink of the beer she offered before setting the bottle on the coffee table.

She set her bottle next to his and angled her body toward him. "We need to finish the conversation we started before you shifted. You have a wolf now, so you can't use that argument against us dating."

He took her hand and scooted closer. "I don't want to have any argument against us dating." He cupped her cheek in his hand, running his thumb across her skin.

Being near him, her entire body hummed, and his dark brown eyes held so much emotion, she couldn't have looked away if she tried. "So don't argue." She drifted toward him.

"I won't." He pressed his lips to hers. They were warm and soft, contrasting with the coarse scruff on his chin, and as she leaned into him, she slid her arms around his shoulders.

An *mmm* resonated in his throat as he coaxed her lips apart with his tongue, and she opened for him willingly, losing herself to the feel of his strong arms wrapped around her. Everything about being with Noah felt right. His scent, his touch, his taste. She couldn't fathom why it had taken her so long to feel the spark, but now, the flame had turned into an inferno.

Yes, this was technically their first "date," but being friends as long as they had, they'd already gone through the *getting to know you* part of a relationship. The only new territory left for her to discover was his body, and she couldn't wait to explore every inch.

Gripping the back of his neck, she rose onto her knees and straddled him. His deep inhale sent a shiver down her spine, and as he glided his hands up and down her back, she slid in closer until she met the bulge in his jeans.

He groaned, gripping her hips, and she moved against him. The friction, even through their clothes, sent a bolt of electricity shooting straight to her core. Good lord, she needed this man.

She slid her hands beneath his shirt, and as her fingers met skin, he sucked in a sharp breath. He was soft flesh over hard muscle. The perfect combination of strength and comfort. Everything she wanted in a mate.

"Amber," he whispered against her lips. "Amber, wait." He clutched her shoulders, breaking the kiss. "Before this goes any further, we need to talk."

"You said you didn't want to argue." She kissed him again, and he moaned, sliding his fingers into her hair.

With a sharp exhale, he pulled away. "It's not my argument we need to discuss. It's yours."

And there was her answer. She didn't feel the tether Odette mentioned because it didn't exist. She slid off him and folded her hands in her lap. "Your wolf hasn't claimed me."

He shook his head. "The guys have described what it feels like, and I...I don't know if I'm capable of it."

"Of course you are; don't be silly."

"I mean it. This wolf inside me doesn't feel like it's mine. He hasn't claimed *me,* so I don't see how he could claim anyone else. *I* have feelings for you. I always have, but this wolf..." He blew out a hard breath. "I don't think you want it tainting the alpha line. There's something wrong with me."

"I don't give a shit about the alpha line, Noah, and there's nothing wrong with you. I wanted you before you had a wolf, and I want you still. You'll get him under control."

"And if I don't?"

"You will." She refused to entertain any other outcome.

He leaned forward, resting his elbows on his knees. "You said yourself Nylah is still alive, so this wolf in me must have been awakened by the Thropynite. Wherever my sister is, she has the stone."

"So? Once we find her, she'll still have the stone. You'll still have your wolf."

"What if this isn't *my* wolf? What if the Thropynite didn't awaken the one inside me? What if its magic fabricated one?"

"That's not..." She grabbed her beer from the table and took a drink. "I don't think..."

"But you don't *know,* and neither do I."

She tipped back her bottle, draining the contents

before returning it to the table. "So where does that leave us? Are you saying you don't want to be with me?"

"No, Amber." He took her hand in both of his. "I'm not saying that at all. I'm saying you shouldn't want to be with me."

*Not this again.* "You don't get to decide what I want."

"Then tell me. Knowing what you know about this wolf and what it's done to you…what do you want?"

"I want you." She laughed as pressure built in the back of her eyes, and she blinked, trying to hold back the tears. "I…" She clamped her mouth shut.

*You know what? Screw it.* She was too old to play games. If he couldn't handle a woman crying over him, it was best she found out now. A tear slid down her cheek. "I have six months to find a mate, or I'll risk bringing shame to my family name. My father could lose his seat on the congress, and Luke… My actions could jeopardize the pack, and I won't allow that to happen. I *will* take a mate by my thirtieth birthday."

"See? I knew you cared about the alpha line."

"I do, and I don't think you'll taint it. You are the only person I can imagine spending the rest of my life with. I think about you constantly when we're apart. When we're together, my blood hums, and I feel like I can't get close enough to you." Another tear slid down her cheek.

"I want to be with you," she continued, "but if you don't feel the same about me, say so. I'm not going to chase you. If you don't want to be with me, I'll move on and look for someone else."

He sat silently, gazing into her eyes, his mouth screwing over to one side as if he didn't know how to break the news. Had she misread the signs? Noah didn't have the best reputation when it came to women. She couldn't recall him having a relationship that lasted longer than a month. Was the passion she felt from him when they kissed merely fabricated? Was it nothing more than the sexual urge of a man for a woman?

He lowered his gaze to their entwined hands, took a deep breath, and let it out slowly. Raising his eyes to meet hers once more, he furrowed his brow. "All I want is to make you happy. I do feel the same, and I do want to be with you."

Her throat thickened, and another tear slid down her cheek. Cupping her face in his hand, he wiped it away with his thumb before leaning in and kissing her. Cool relief flooded her body, but as she tried to move closer to him, he pulled away.

"There's still the issue with this wolf. What are we going to do if he doesn't claim you?"

Her heart ached at the thought. Maybe she should take Odette up on her offer of praying to the Voodoo loa of love. Perhaps there was some sort of spell that would convince the wolf she belonged with him.

Who was she kidding? Magic couldn't force a fate-bound bond. The future of her relationship was up to fate itself. "How about we take it one day at a time? I don't see any reason why we can't enjoy each other's company while you're getting your wolf under control." She slid her hand up his thigh.

"If I get him under control, and he still doesn't claim you?" He placed his hand on top of hers.

"We'll cross that bridge when we get to it."

He folded his arms over his chest. "You mean you'll leave me."

She sighed. "I refuse to be the reason you live your life without a fate-bound. If your wolf doesn't claim me, we can't be together, but I don't want to focus on that right now."

"Neither do I, but…" He froze and clutched his stomach. "Oh, shit."

"What's wrong?"

The tendons in his neck protruded like he was straining, and a sinking sensation formed in Amber's core. Sweat beaded on his forehead as he ground his teeth.

"Is it?" She gripped the arm of the sofa.

He nodded. "Run."

She shot to her feet and darted around to the back of the couch.

"I can't stop it," he mumbled a moment before he transformed into a wolf.

The beast locked his gaze on Amber, and her blood fell from her head to her feet. "Not again." She shuffled backward, trying her damnedest not to make any sudden movements. Noah was in there somewhere. He wouldn't try to attack her again.

The wolf growled, baring his massive teeth, and Amber's back met the wall behind her. "Hey, buddy. I'm supposed to be your fate-bound. Don't you recognize me?" She inched toward the bedroom door, her heart frantically pounding against her ribs. "Tell him, Noah."

Narrowing his eyes, the wolf snarled.

"Or not."

The wolf climbed onto the couch, his enormous paws resting on the back pillows as he glared at her. This felt like the exact opposite of being claimed as a mate. He rocked back onto his haunches, and she darted into the bedroom before he could spring, slamming the door so hard, it bounced back open without latching.

If she'd have thought this through, she'd have headed

out the front door rather than trapping herself in a room with no exit, but here she was, backed into a corner. A thud sounded from the living room as the wolf's paws hit wood, and her heart lodged in her throat.

He lurked in the doorway, and a low growl reverberated through the room. He prowled toward her, moving slowly. All he'd have to do was lunge and she'd be dead, if not from his teeth, then from the heart attack that was about to take her under.

Her gaze never straying from the wolf, she fumbled with her nightstand, gripping a lamp to defend herself. He growled, crouching low and inching toward her. She tossed the lamp aside, drawing his attention toward the window, and scrambled over the bed, racing out of the room and pulling the door shut behind her.

Now he finally lunged. He hit the door with a *bang* and howled, scratching at the wood when he couldn't bust it open. Amber gripped the knob, pulling with all her weight to keep it closed as she fished her phone from her pocket and dialed her brother. Luke answered on the third ring.

"It happened again," she said through clenched teeth. "Noah shifted. He's locked in my bedroom."

"Are you okay?"

"Yeah, he didn't attack, but he is not a happy wolf."

"I'm on my way."

---

This was insane. One minute, Noah was talking to Amber about the possibility of building a future together, and the next, this goddamn beast had taken over, scaring the shit out of her again.

The wolf snarled, slamming his shoulder into the door to get to her. The beast wasn't connected to him on a soul level, so Noah couldn't decipher exactly what he was feeling. Based on the howls and growls, his guess was rage.

"Noah, I know you're in there," Amber's voice drifted through the wood. "You need to take back control. You've done it before, so I know you can do it again."

God, how he wanted to. If he could get this fucking wolf under control, he could spend his time convincing Amber she didn't need to be his fate-bound. The man loved her enough to be happy. If only she could be happy with him.

"It's open," she called, and heavy footsteps sounded on the hardwood floor.

The wolf let out a low growl, his ears flattening against his head as he sensed the alpha's presence. Luke pounded on the door. "Noah, get your wolf under control and shift. That's an order."

He fought to gain dominance, but the wolf refused to let go. It tossed its head back, issuing a long, pained howl.

"Right now, Noah," Luke commanded. "If he can't shift, I'll have to go in and subdue him," he said to Amber.

"Noah, please," she pleaded. "You can do this. I know you can."

Her voice seemed to soothe the beast. Maybe it just soothed the man, but either way, the wolf relinquished control, and he shifted to his human form. He raked his hands through his hair, fisting them and pulling at the roots.

The growl this time came from his own throat, and as the door opened, he whirled around, making Amber flinch. "Goddammit! I'm sorry, Amber. I don't know why this keeps happening."

"I guess it's safe to say your wolf won't be claiming me anytime soon." Her lips curved into a sad smile and flattened again as she lowered her gaze.

Luke stood behind her with his arms crossed. "Until it does, you two are not to be alone together."

Amber spun around to face him. "I'll be alone with him if I want to be alone with him. Big Brother doesn't get to run my life."

"But your alpha makes the rules when it comes to the wolves." He softened his gaze. "I'm only thinking about your safety."

"Thanks, but I can take care of myself."

He blew out a frustrated breath. "Okay, then imagine how Noah would feel if his wolf harmed you. Do you want to put that on him?"

"I…" She looked at Noah, and sadness filled her eyes. "No, I don't."

"I'm going to make a phone call. You two wait here." Luke turned on his heel and strode out of the bedroom.

"I'm so sorry." Noah moved toward Amber but hesitated. His wolf must've scared the daylights out of her, so he doubted she'd want to be anywhere near him.

"It's not your fault." She stepped into his embrace, wrapping her arms around his waist and holding him tight. "We're going to figure this out."

Noah closed his eyes, memorizing the way she felt pressed against him. He'd hugged her hundreds of times since they were kids, but now, knowing she cared for him the way he cared for her, holding her made an ache spread through his body that felt so good, it was almost painful… nearly unbearable.

He nuzzled against the side of her head, breathing in her sweet floral scent. "What if it is my fault?"

"What do you mean?"

"If Nylah is alive, the only way I'd gain the ability to shift would be from the Thropynite, and I knew she was trying to find it. I could have done something to stop her from bringing it here."

"No. Shh…" She leaned back, holding his face in her hands. "It is not your fault. If I were in your place, if I were Luke's twin and couldn't shift, I'd do anything it takes to make it right. Fate dealt you a bad hand. You and Nylah did what you had to do to fix it."

"Amber…"

She brushed her lips to his. Her soft, gentle kiss warmed him to his core, and while he had no idea what his wolf felt at the moment, the man felt an overwhelming urge to protect her. Luke was right; they couldn't be together unchaperoned. It wasn't worth the risk.

"Ahem." Luke stood in the doorway, sympathy pinching his brow as he looked at them.

Amber turned to face her brother, keeping one arm wrapped around Noah's waist. As Luke's gaze flicked between them, she rested her hand on Noah's chest, answering the unspoken question hanging in the air.

Noah made eye contact with Luke, his own silent question causing nausea to churn in his gut. With Amber's position in the pack, their feelings for each other wouldn't matter if the alpha didn't approve.

Luke held his gaze for what felt like an eternity before looking at Amber. Her grip tightened around Noah's waist, and Luke returned his gaze to Noah. The alpha inhaled deeply, and Noah held his breath. As he exhaled, Luke nodded once, and cool relief unfurled on Noah's core. One hurdle had been crossed. Now, he just had to convince his unruly wolf to claim her.

"I'm sending you to the congress for an examination," Luke said.

Noah swallowed hard. He was one step closer to his secret being spilled, and who knew what kind of punishment the congress would deal? "They believe Nylah is dead?"

"They do."

Amber sensed his unease and patted his chest. "When do we leave?"

"You're not going," Luke said.

"The hell I'm not." She released her hold on Noah and moved toward her brother. "I'm not leaving his side. Besides, I can make myself useful. I'll scour the archives for information about the Grunch and the stone. They may believe Nylah is dead, but Noah and I know she's not. We're going to find her."

"I don't want you near him without an alpha present."

"Then come with us."

"I won't leave the pack while a murderer is on the loose. Whether it's a Grunch or not, it's obviously supernatural. Dad's driving out tomorrow to pick him up."

Amber sighed, irritated. "Dad is an alpha. Every member of the congress is a retired alpha. You'll have to come up with a better argument than that to keep me here."

Luke's jaw tightened. "All right, but you're both staying at Mom and Dad's."

She placed a hand on Luke's shoulder and kissed his cheek. "I'll start packing."

Noah fought his smile. Amber's strength and determination were two of the things he loved about her.

"Say your goodbyes. I'm going home, and so is Noah." Luke returned to the living room.

"I'll see you tomorrow." Amber hugged him and gave him a quick kiss on the lips.

He was tempted to lean in for more. Now that he had her, he couldn't get enough of her, but it was best not to keep the alpha waiting. Luke had approved both their relationship and their going to the congress together. He didn't need to press his luck.

"Until then." He tucked her hair behind her ear, pressing his lips to her forehead before heading out the door.

Cicadas chirped in the trees above, their shrill song greeting him as he stepped into the warm night air. A couple lounged on the porch of the neighboring house, and a dog barked from across the street.

Pausing in the driveway, Noah turned to Luke. "Can I ask you a personal question?"

He arched a brow. "You can ask. I might not answer."

"Fair enough." He glanced toward the house where Amber waved from the window. He returned the wave, and she disappeared behind the curtain. "What does it feel like when you find your fate-bound? How do you know?"

Luke pressed his lips into a hard line and glanced at the house. "If she was yours, you wouldn't have to ask."

# CHAPTER FIFTEEN

"Come in, come in. It's so good to see you." Amber's mom passed her up, pulling Noah into a tight hug instead. "I'm so sorry about Nylah." She wrapped her arm around his shoulders, guiding him into the living room.

"It's good to see you too, Mom," Amber said under her breath, and she turned to her father. She'd held her tongue on the drive over, not wanting to bring up her failed "dates" in front of Noah. Now, she had to put her foot down. Otherwise, her parents would probably send fertility spells disguised as sweet tea as soon as she mated. "I don't appreciate you meddling in my affairs. Sending those men to meet me was out of line."

He shook his head and patted her back as if she were a little girl. "It's the security of the pack I was concerned about, sweetheart."

"Of course," she muttered. "My happiness doesn't matter as long as I continue the alpha line." Amber moved toward the living room, while her dad disappeared into his study. She took a deep breath, bracing herself for her mother's form of meddling—which didn't seem so bad compared to her dad's—and strode toward an accent chair.

Her mom caught her hand, and, making a *tsk* sound, she ushered her toward the couch next to Noah.

*I'm going to strangle you for this, Luke.* Her brother was such a tattletale.

"How are you two holding up?" Debbie asked. "How are your parents, Noah?"

He glanced at Amber. "They're holding onto hope."

"Nylah isn't dead, Mom."

"How do you know? Your father said—"

"I just do. Trust me on this. I can feel it, okay?" She gave her mom a pointed look.

"Oh, that's good news, isn't it?" She looked toward the study, but Amber's dad had closed the door. "You'll share details when you can?"

Amber nodded, thankful her mom so easily dropped the subject, while simultaneously bracing herself for the next inevitable line of questioning.

"So, then, tell me what's new with you, Noah." Debbie leaned forward in her seat and patted him on the knee.

Noah chuckled. "You mean besides suddenly inheriting the ability to shift?"

"Yes, besides that." Her mom waved off his comment, grinning from ear to ear and cutting her gaze between them. "Oh, I can't stand it. I wanted you to say it first, but…congratulations, you two. Luke told me."

Noah's eyes widened, and his hands curled into fists in his lap.

Amber closed her eyes for a long blink, letting out a slow exhale. "What exactly did he tell you?"

"Well, that you're together. I can't wait to start planning the wedding."

"We, umm..." Noah gave Amber a desperate look. Poor guy. *Way to scare him off, Mom.*

Her mother's smile faded. "Did he...? Is it not true?"

"We're dating." Amber placed her hand on top of Noah's fist, and he relaxed with her touch. "That's all for now, Mom." She flashed another pointed look at her, hoping she'd take the hint.

In typical Debbie style, she did not. "Nonsense. You've been best friends since you were knee high to a cicada. If romance is sparking after all this time, you'll be mates before you know it."

Amber's dad strode into the room and cleared his throat. "The congress is ready for you, Noah. Amber, would you like to tag along?"

"Absolutely." She started to argue that she wouldn't be *tagging* anywhere—that she had work to do—but she was thankful for the distraction from her mother's prying, so she kept her mouth shut.

"I'll have dinner ready for you when you get home," her mother said. "I'm making my famous meatloaf for Noah."

"Mmm..." Noah said as he rose to his feet. "Thank you, Mrs. Mason. It's been a minute since I've had your meatloaf. I'm looking forward to it."

Outside, Amber climbed into the back seat of her dad's jet-black Silverado, and they headed toward the werewolf national congress headquarters. Luckily, her dad didn't ask any questions about her relationship with Noah. She didn't want to think about what would happen if his wolf didn't claim her.

Instead, they rode in silence. Her dad's gaze remained

glued to the road, while Noah stole glances at her through the side mirror. Amber leaned her head against the cool glass, offering him the best smile she could fake while her mind whirred with what-ifs. Until last night, she'd been confident Noah could get his wolf under control, but what if he couldn't?

What if Luke's nod of approval had merely been his way of warding off another forced shift? Both times Noah's wolf had taken control, they had been discussing their relationship, and both times, the beast had stalked her. What if that was the animal's way of telling them they weren't meant to be? Or what if the congress had other plans for Noah and tried to remove him from the pack? They'd have to go rogue to be together if that were the case, and going rogue was something Amber could never do.

Or could she?

Her vision blurred as she gazed out the window at the trees whizzing past, and nausea churned in her gut. There was no need to get worked up about this now. She had no control over what the congress would decide about him, and her energy was best focused on things she *could* do.

Gravel crunched beneath the tires as they pulled off the main road onto a narrow path only wide enough for a single vehicle. A car approaching from the opposite direction had to pull over halfway into the ditch, while her dad did the same as they passed. Oak trees lined both sides of the road, creating a tunnel effect, their branches reaching out to tangle with their neighbors'.

Amber swallowed the bile from the back of her throat. She had the foreboding sense that she was being led to her doom, which was absolutely ridiculous. It didn't feel like a premonition, and her father wouldn't bring her here if she'd be in any sort of danger. She'd simply watched too many horror movies for her own good. From now on, movie night would consist of romantic comedies only.

An eight-foot stone wall surrounded the property as they approached, and an iron gate blocked the entrance. Damn, this wasn't how she imagined the congress at all. She'd pictured a cabin in the woods with maybe a subterranean tunnel system where they housed the archives.

The gate rolled open, and her father pulled into the driveway of a massive nineteenth-century colonial mansion, complete with columns and a long gallery on the second floor. He stopped the truck at the top of the U-shaped drive, and a valet scurried out to open his door.

Amber stifled a laugh. Her father was *so* not the being-waited-on type. Noah opened her door, and she slid out, gripping his hand like this was the last time she'd get to touch him.

"Everything you are about to see is to remain in strictest confidence," her dad said as if reciting a speech written by someone else. "Amber, what you find in the archives must be discussed with Luke before the information is disseminated to the pack, and Noah…" He glanced at her before looking into Noah's eyes. "What happens in the congress's chambers stays in the chambers."

*Thanks, Dad. Not helping with the overbearing sense of impending doom.* "Can I talk to you in private for a second?" She squeezed Noah's hand and released it before lacing her arm around her dad's elbow and walking him out of earshot. "Is Noah in danger being here? They won't…do anything to him, will they?"

Her dad missed a beat in his reply, and something strange flashed in his eyes before he composed his answer.

"They're just going to examine him right now." He patted her hand and gestured toward the entrance.

*Yeah... Not helping at all.*

Inside, a crystal chandelier hung in the foyer, and hardwood floors stretched down a long hallway. A man around Amber's age sat at a desk in a small room to the left, and when he saw her father, he shot to his feet.

"The witch is getting set up, Mr. Mason," he said. "It'll be a few more minutes."

"Witch?" Amber clutched her father's arm and lowered her voice to a whisper. "You said they were only examining him."

He glanced at her hand on his arm before giving her a sharp look, reminding her that, while he may be her father, in here, he was a congresswolf and should be treated as such. "Let's get you to the archives, and then I'll take Noah to the examination room."

Amber released her hold, taking Noah's hand instead, and followed her father down the hall and up a staircase to the second floor. A line of windows revealed the back courtyard, where stone benches surrounded a fountain and topiaries trimmed into the shapes of wolves dotted the grounds.

The wood floor creaked with their footsteps, and as her dad opened a set of double doors, Amber's breath caught at the sight of the archives. Row after row of floor-to-ceiling bookcases lined the dimly lit space, their shelves filled with antique volumes and boxes of who knew what.

"This is my daughter," he said to the woman behind a raised counter. "She has permission to use the archives." He turned to Amber. "Cynthia will help you get started."

Amber pulled Noah into a hug. He was tense, but as

she nuzzled into his neck, brushing her lips over his skin, he relaxed a little. "I'll be here when you're done."

He pulled back, running his thumb over her cheek before pressing a piece of paper into her hand. "I'll see you soon."

"Noah." Her dad stood halfway down the hall, so Noah gave her a half-smile, turned, and walked away.

Amber stepped into the archives and unfolded the paper to find the note Nylah left him when she started working for the congress. She quickly folded it and shoved it into her pocket. "Hi, Cynthia, I'm Amber."

"Hi." She scurried from around the counter, the heels of her patent leather pumps clicking on the floor. A black pencil skirt brushed the tops of her knees, and a light blue silk blouse perfectly matched her eyes. "I'm second-born as well. What's your ability?"

"Empathic premonitions. You?"

"Finding lost things…and people."

Amber's pulse thrummed. "You can find missing people?"

"Usually." She gestured to a table in the center of the room and moved toward it. "You're looking for Nylah L'Eveque, right? She was from your pack."

"Yes. Can you find her?"

Cynthia shook her head, and her blonde curls swished around her face. "I've tried."

"Will you try again?"

"I need an item that belonged to the missing person. Clothing, jewelry, a journal. Anything that had meaning to them. I sat in Nylah's room, surrounded by her possessions, and I couldn't locate her, so I doubt—"

"Will you try one more time? I have a letter she

wrote." She pulled the note from her pocket, offering it to Cynthia.

"One more time." Cynthia took the note and flashed a sympathetic smile as she began to unfold the paper.

Amber put her hand on the letter. "It's private." Noah had given it to her so the congress wouldn't find it. She had no idea if she could trust Cynthia to keep his secret.

"Of course." She refolded the letter, clutching it in both hands as she closed her eyes and inhaled deeply.

Amber stared at her, willing an image of Nylah's location to come to her mind. The seconds stretched into excruciatingly long minutes before Cynthia finally opened her eyes.

"Nothing." She handed the letter back to Amber. "It's as if she no longer exists."

"What does that mean? She didn't just vanish into thin air."

Cynthia pursed her lips. "Usually when this happens, it's because…" She cringed before finishing, "It's because the body has been decimated. Turned to ash and spread in the wind."

Amber's stomach sank, and she touched a hand to a bookshelf to steady herself. "No. She can't be dead. I can feel that she's alive, and so can Noah."

"And I can't feel her at all." Cynthia drew her shoulders toward her ears. "But that's why you're here, right? To see what you can find out about the Grunch she was investigating. Come on; I've already pulled some volumes."

Amber followed Cynthia to the table where a stack of books lay on the corner. "Do you have any information about the Thropynite?"

"I'll see what I can find." Cynthia scurried away, and Amber dove into the books.

She started with a thick, leather-bound volume filled with handwritten pages dated 1729. The paper smelled old and musty, and as she flipped the delicate pages, she found an entry documenting the Grunch. She scoured the book before moving on to the next. After two hours of reading, she hadn't gleaned any more information about the gargoyle creatures than what she already knew.

And the Thropynite... Two different entries about the stone stated the person had to have physical contact with it for the magic to activate. If that were the case, it simply being in New Orleans couldn't possibly be the reason Noah could shift. And if the Thropynite had nothing to do with his newfound ability, that could only mean Nylah was dead.

So what was this nagging feeling both she and Noah had that she was still alive? Could they both be imagining it? She was about to give in to defeat when Cynthia brought one more book.

"I found this one. It's an account written by a witch who was supposedly held captive by the Grunch, so I don't know how much merit it has. The creatures killed magical beings. I doubt they would have kept her alive, but here it is." She set the thin book on the table in front of Amber and took the seat next to her. "Have you found anything useful?"

"Not yet." Amber opened the book and read the witch's account. Her eyes widened as she took in the story, her pulse thrumming in her ears. Her knee bounced beneath the table, and when she finished the short report, she gently closed the book. "While I'm here, would you mind finding the records of how the Crescent City Wolf Pack was formed? I'd like to read our history."

"Absolutely." Cynthia stood and disappeared behind a shelf.

Amber waited a beat or two until her new friend was far enough away before pulling out her phone and snapping pictures of the pages in the witch's book. It was all here, in vivid detail, right down to the leader of the Grunch's name. If the account were true, she knew where Nylah was *and* why Noah inherited the ability to shift.

---

Noah's stomach soured as he followed his former alpha into the exam room. He'd expected to meet in the congress's chambers to be questioned by the lot of them. Instead, Mr. Mason gestured for him to enter a small room near the kitchen on the first floor. The scents of bleach and patchouli mingled in the air, creating a sickening smell that coated the inside of his nose and reached all the way down to his throat. He swallowed the rancid taste from his mouth and stepped inside.

A hospital bed stood in the center of the room. Leather shackles for his arms and legs lay open on the surface, and a woman in her mid-fifties with long black hair and bright green eyes stood in the corner.

Instinct forced Noah to retreat, and he backed into Mr. Mason's chest. He clutched Noah's arms. "This is Helga. She'll be conducting the exam." He pointed to a large rectangular mirror on the wall. "I'll be watching from the next room. Try to relax."

*Yeah, right.* Even the toughest alpha couldn't relax if he were chained to a bed, and he had a hunch those leather straps were reinforced with magic. Regular hospital restraints would be no match for the strength of a shifter.

"Do I have to be tied down?" He sat on the edge of the bed.

Mr. Mason gestured for him to lie on his back. "It's for Helga's safety. She's going to ask you to shift, and these restraints have been bespelled to remain intact and hold your wolf."

Noah ground his teeth as he lay back and let them strap him to the bed. Magic tingled on his wrists and ankles, and he rested his head on a thin pillow. The shackles gave him enough room to sit up, but he could only lift his arms halfway to his shoulders.

"I'll be in at the first sign of trouble." Mr. Mason nodded and left the room, closing the door behind him, the lock sliding into place sounding like a nail in a coffin. What had he gotten himself into?

Helga drifted to the end of the bed and hovered her hands above Noah's head. "Lie still."

He lifted his chained wrists. "I don't have much of a choice."

She shook her head, chiding him. "Can you sense your wolf? Describe what you feel."

"I can feel it's there, but that's about it. I don't have a clue about its emotions or what thoughts are running through its mind. I can call it to the surface to shift, but it's hard to regain control to shift back. It feels like it's not mine."

She clutched the sides of his head and hummed low in her throat. Her magic pricked at his skin like static, and her nails digging into his scalp reminded him of the carnage the Grunch had committed. He inhaled deeply, trying to calm his racing heart.

"It's strong, and it's yours. You have a block, though." She released her grip and drifted toward a table filled with glass bottles, dried herbs, and copper containers. She crushed some herbs with a mortar and pestle and mixed them with a yellow liquid in a bowl before bringing it to his bedside.

"Drink this." She offered it to him.

He hesitated, eyeing the bowl and arching a brow. "What is it?"

"A potion to open your mind." She grabbed his hand and shoved the bowl into his grasp. "Drink it."

He gazed at the steaming concoction and curled his lip. No way in hell was he consuming this without knowing what it was. "You want me to take drugs. What's in it? Is it LSD? Mushrooms?"

"It's magic." The witch huffed and glared at the two-way mirror.

"Drink the potion, Noah," Mr. Mason's voice boomed over the intercom.

Noah knew better than to disobey an alpha—especially one with a seat on the congress—so he pressed the bowl to his lips and swallowed the syrupy liquid. There was definitely some kind of root in there, as he could taste the earth and the sharp, bitter flavor of mold. He fought the urge to gag and handed the bowl to the witch before lying back and closing his eyes.

His head spun, the magic instantly taking hold and making him dizzy as all get-out. His stomach lurched, and he coughed, rolling to his side in case his lunch decided to make a reappearance.

Helga began chanting, either in a language he didn't understand, or the drugs were making her speech sound foreign. He couldn't tell which. The air in the room thickened, buzzing with electricity as the witch's magic built. She clutched his head again, rolling him onto his back and sending a jolt of energy straight through his skull and into his brain.

He was falling. Darkness consumed him for a moment before stars glittered all around. Then he splashed down into a sea of inky blue, the water flowing over his head until it was impossible to breathe. He struggled in his mind, swimming toward a light above the surface, but the harder he kicked, the farther away the light seemed.

As he hung weightlessly in the empty abyss, an image formed in his mind. Amber's sweet smile danced behind his eyes, and he rose, breaking the surface and gasping for breath.

"Now shift," the witch's voice grated in his ears.

He shook his head, squeezing his eyes shut and willing Amber's face to stay in his view. If the potion made him see her, there had to be a reason.

"Shift, Noah. That's an order." Mr. Mason's voice filled the room, and he was compelled to obey.

He called on the beast, *his* wolf, according to the witch, and he transformed. The wolf snarled, standing on the bed, the shackles magically tightening around his legs. He locked his gaze on the witch, and though Noah struggled to gain control, he was nothing more than a subconscious energy going along for the ride. The wolf rocked back before springing toward her.

The restraints held, and the bed toppled over, sending the wolf crashing to the floor. He scrambled to his paws and lunged again, dragging the bed as he prowled toward her. Noah tried to take over. He willed his body to shift, but the potion had rendered him powerless against the beast.

The door swung open a moment before Mr. Mason shifted and barreled toward him. The alpha growled, a deep vibration resonating from his chest, and placed himself between the witch and Noah's wolf, baring his teeth and looming toward him.

Thank the heavens Luke had trained the wolf to submit. He lay on his belly, resting his head on his paws and letting out a low whine. As the wolf relinquished control to the alpha, Noah grabbed on and forced the beast to release his hold.

Returning to his human form, Noah sat on the floor, unable to stand due to the restraints. "I'm sorry," he said to both Helga and the alpha.

Mr. Mason shifted and knelt beside him. "Are you in control now?"

"Yes, sir." He lowered his head.

They removed the restraints, and Noah helped Mr. Mason right the fallen bed before he led them into an office next door. Noah sank into a wooden chair while Helga and Mr. Mason conversed.

"What's the verdict?" the alpha asked.

Helga frowned at Noah. "The wolf belongs to him, as I said. However, it has not joined with his soul. This is why he lacks control."

"Any idea how this happened?"

"The wolf should not have been awakened. I sense magic was involved, which made the transformation go awry."

Mr. Mason's brows slammed down over his eyes. "Do you know anything about this?"

Noah's heart sank into his stomach. How much longer could he keep his secret? "Both Amber and I feel like Nylah is alive somewhere. That's all I know." He lowered his gaze to his lap, afraid the alpha could sense his lie.

"Do you know of a way to fuse the wolf to his soul?"

"You must find the magic that awakened it. It can either solve the problem or put the wolf to rest for good."

"In this condition, can the wolf claim a mate?" Mr. Mason asked.

"He wouldn't know it if it did." She clasped her hands in front of her. "He'll be a danger to any mate he might choose."

"Thank you, Helga. Please submit your report to the archives."

The witch nodded and left the room. Noah gripped his thighs, digging his fingertips into his muscles. He couldn't make himself breathe, so he sat there holding the end of his exhale, unable to move. Amber would never be safe around him. Not only had his selfish desire to awaken his wolf brought a reign of terror on New Orleans, but now he'd destroyed any chance he had at a life with the one person who mattered most.

Mr. Mason stood in front of him with his arms crossed. "Whatever relationship you have with my daughter ends now. I won't have you endangering her life."

Noah agreed.

## CHAPTER SIXTEEN

Amber slipped her phone into her pocket as Cynthia returned with the books she'd requested. She smiled and thanked her before flipping one open and staring at the page, but her eyes didn't register the words. Instead, her thoughts raced in a thousand different directions as she chewed her bottom lip.

It all made sense now: Noah gaining the ability to shift, his wolf not wanting to obey him, why she was certain Nylah was alive. It was all she could do to keep from bursting out of the archives and intruding on the council's examination of Noah. She didn't need a witch to tell her what was going on with him; it was all recorded right here in this journal.

Her knee bounced incessantly beneath the table, and as the heavy door swung open and her father entered the room, she shot to her feet and started toward him. But she froze midstride when Noah didn't follow him in. "Where is he?" Her voice held accusation, and her father stiffened.

"He's waiting in the truck. Let's go home." He turned

and strode out the door, leaving Amber standing there with her mouth open.

"What happened in the examination? Is he okay?" She jogged to catch up with her dad.

"The congress will be meeting tomorrow afternoon to discuss his affliction, so I'll be taking you both home first thing in the morning. That's all I can say."

"What do you mean that's all you can say?" She followed him down the stairs and out the front door, her heart running at a thousand miles a minute. "Dad, what are you not telling me? I'm part of the alpha line; I have a right to know. Or is that fact only convenient when you want it to be?"

He stopped, taking her biceps in his hands. "Your relationship with Noah ends today. He is not a welcome addition to our family."

She scoffed, opening and closing her mouth as she tried to find the words. "Are you serious? Mom has been on me nonstop to hook up with him, and now you're forbidding me from dating him?"

"That was before his affliction." His gaze softened, and he squeezed her arms before letting her go. "He's been deemed an unfit mate."

"Unfit? Why? Because his wolf is wild?" This couldn't be happening. They didn't come all this way with the intent to help Noah, only to have the national congress of werewolves say he was unfit to be her mate. No way. She refused to accept it. "I found something in the archives that expl—"

"Drop it, Amber. My decision is final." He gave her a pointed look, the same look he gave her when she was a kid and had been pressing her luck. The look that meant the conversation was over, end of story.

But this story was just beginning. "Don't you want to hear what I found in the archives?"

He sighed heavily. "Report your findings to Luke when you get home tomorrow. I don't *meddle* in your pack's affairs."

"No, you just want to control your children. First Luke's life, and now mine. Things are changing, Dad. You have to accept that—"

"Your mother has dinner waiting for us." He cut her off as if she were nothing more than a belligerent teenager and gestured to the truck where Noah sat in the passenger seat, staring out the front window.

"Noah." She ran to the truck and pulled on the handle, but his door was locked. She knocked on the window, and he looked at her with sad eyes, shaking his head.

With a groan, she climbed into the back seat, but before she could speak to him, her father joined them, silencing their would-be conversation. Amber buckled her seatbelt and clenched her teeth. Noah would talk to her; she just had to get him alone.

Country music playing quietly through the speakers softened the heavy silence hanging in the Chevy on the fifteen-minute drive to her parents' home. Neither her father nor Noah said a word, and Amber chewed the inside of her cheek, her dad's verdict playing on a loop in her mind. *Noah has been deemed an unfit mate.* That was total bullshit, and if her stubborn old man would allow her to explain what she'd found, he would feel otherwise.

She seethed with anger. She—and only she—would decide who was fit to be her mate. Noah was a better fit than any man she'd ever met.

Her mom was putting dinner on the table as they

walked through the front door, and she smiled, oblivious to the news Amber had just received. She set it up so Amber would sit next to Noah, and her dad inhaled, opening his mouth as if to protest the arrangement. When her mom cocked her head, he sighed and took his seat. Amber sank into her chair and gave Noah a small smile, which he didn't return.

"How did the examination go?" her mom asked. "I hope all is well."

Noah cleared his throat and looked at her dad.

"Yes, Father." Amber folded her hands on the table. "What happened in the examination?"

He narrowed his eyes at her before addressing her mom. "We'll discuss it later." He shoved a piece of meatloaf into his mouth.

They ate in silence, the tension in the room so thick it rivaled the mashed potatoes. Amber slid her leg toward Noah, leaning it outward so her knee touched his. He swallowed hard and then shifted in his seat, moving his leg away from hers.

Amber's heart ached. No doubt her father had put the fear of God in him. The man was old-fashioned at best. He bought into the old ways, where the men's— especially the elders'—word was law no matter how irrational it may be.

Under Luke's command, the Crescent City Wolf Pack was finally seeing the light of the twenty-first century. No one—not her dad, not a bunch of old fogies in the congress—was going to send them back to the Dark Ages.

As they finished dinner, Noah stood and picked up his empty plate.

"Leave it," her mom said. "I'll take care of the dishes."

Noah returned his plate to the table, glancing at

Amber before looking at her mom. "Thank you for dinner, Mrs. Mason. It was delicious."

She smiled warmly. "Any time, dear."

"I'm going to turn in early if that's all right."

"You two can take the big bedroom at the end of the hall upstairs." She gave Amber a conspiratorial wink.

"They'll be taking separate rooms," her dad said.

Her mom gave her a quizzical look. "Okay… Amber, you can have the second room on the right, then."

"Thank you." Noah pushed in his chair and strode out of the dining room without a second glance.

"I'll be in my study." Her dad stood there for a moment, but if he was expecting a goodnight from her, he would be sorely disappointed. She couldn't even look at the man.

As her father left, Amber picked up the plates and followed her mom into the kitchen. She waited until she heard the study door click shut, and they both turned to each other, speaking at once. Amber closed her mouth, letting her mom go first.

"What the devil is going on? It would have taken a butcher knife to chop through the tension in there."

Amber set the plates in the sink and turned on the water, just in case her old man was listening. "He has decided Noah is unfit to be my mate."

"What?" Her mom's mouth fell open. "That's the most ridiculous thing I've ever heard. You two are perfect for each other. What happened during the examination?"

"I have no idea. He won't tell me anything, except that my relationship with Noah is over. Will you talk to him?"

"Of course I will, but I don't know that it will do much good. You know how stubborn your father can be.

Have you talked to Noah about this? What does he think?"

"I haven't been alone with him to ask. He barely looks at me." A sob bubbled up from her chest, but she caught it in her throat and blinked back the tears that threatened to spill.

"Oh, honey." Her mom pulled her into a hug. "I'm on your side. I'll get your father to come to bed early so you can talk to Noah."

"Thanks, Mom. You're the best."

---

Noah lay in the center of the queen-sized bed, staring at the ceiling fan whirring above. He'd felt his fair share of humiliation lately, but being called an unfit mate took the cake. He could hardly look Amber in the eye, much less have a conversation with her about it.

Anger fumed in his soul. She should have listened to him in the beginning when he told her she deserved better. His wolf awakening had given him the false hope that he might be able to be the mate she needed, and he'd let his guard down, allowing himself to fall completely head over tail for her.

And look where that landed him. Forbidden from taking a mate. Forbidden from love.

He growled and rolled onto his side, cursing his goddamn wolf for emerging when it did, cursing Nylah for finding the Thropynite, cursing himself for not stopping her. He could have accepted his fate and given up on the dream of becoming a shifter, but no. He'd been selfish. He'd put his sister's life in danger, and he'd almost killed Amber twice.

No, he did not deserve Amber or anyone, for that matter. He didn't deserve the air he breathed.

A light knock sounded on the door a moment before Amber stepped through. She wore a pale pink satin nightgown, and the moonlight streaming in through the window gave her fair skin an ethereal glow.

His entire body ached at the sight of her, his throat thickening as she glided across the room and sank onto the edge of the bed. He pushed to a sitting position, leaning his back against the headboard and forcing himself to look into her eyes.

"We need to talk." She folded one leg beneath her, angling her body to face him, her phone clutched in her hand.

"I know." He inhaled deeply before blowing out a hard breath. "I told you from the beginning I couldn't be the wolf you need."

"Stop it, okay? None of you know what I need better than me, so I don't want to hear any more of that. Tell me what happened during the examination."

"It was just me and a witch alone in a room with your dad watching through a window. She made me drink this potion that let her look into my psyche, and then I had to shift." His jaw clenched at the memory.

When he didn't elaborate, Amber rested her hand on his leg. "What happened then?"

He let out a sardonic laugh. "If I hadn't been chained to the bed with magical shackles... My wolf tried to attack, so your dad busted in and forced me to shift back to human. When it was over, the witch told your dad that being with me would put you in danger."

He shrugged and toyed with a loose thread in the sheet. "So here we are. I could be thrown in the pit just for being alone with you right now." Not that he cared. It was worth the risk to tell her a proper goodbye.

"First of all, we're not alone. My parents are asleep downstairs. Second, are you saying my dad is the only congresswolf who knows about the examination? No one else was there?"

"It was just the witch and your dad."

"So the congress hasn't deemed you an unfit mate. That's all my dad's doing." She laughed cynically. "Typical. It's just like my father to make a life-altering decision and expect everyone else to follow along."

"Once he meets with them tomorrow, I'm sure they'll agree. I'm a danger to everyone, and it's only a matter of time before they connect the dots and figure out I'm shifting because of the Thropynite and Nylah is the one who brought it here. She's better off never being found if they discover our secret."

"You're not shifting because of the stone. You'd have to make physical contact with it for its magic to affect you. Look at this." She offered him her phone, and he gazed at the image of an elegant script on a withered page.

"What is this?" He flipped through the photos, taking in page after page that she'd photographed.

"It's a witch's explanation of what happened to the Grunch. She claims the Grunch live in a pocket dimension, just outside our plane. Alrick, their leader, held her captive for a century, the magic of the dimension slowing time so she hardly aged. She managed to escape, and she stole the piece of Thropynite they'd brought here. She created a potion to destroy the stone, which froze them all in their dimension."

He furrowed his brow as he read the account. "If this

is true, it's proof that Nylah *did* find the Thropynite. How will this help?"

"I think the Grunch have Nylah. If she's trapped in their pocket dimension, she has ceased to exist on this plane. Since she no longer exists here, your wolf was awakened, but because she hasn't actually passed on, your wolf can't fuse with your soul."

He stared into her bright blue eyes as he processed her words. So much hope filled them, he couldn't help but believe it was true. "That would explain why we both feel like she's alive, despite the evidence that she isn't."

She beamed a smile. "It makes perfect sense."

"When she retrieved the stone from overseas, it awakened the Grunch, and they took her while she was investigating their reappearance."

"She probably had no idea the Thropynite would awaken the monsters; no one even knew they were here. If we can find Nylah…"

"We'll find the stone."

"And the stone can fuse your wolf with your soul." She took his hand. "Then no one can say you're an unfit mate."

"And you found all this out while a witch was poking around in my mind." He laughed. "You're amazing."

"No one has to know what we're doing. I know a witch who will help us with the spell to disintegrate the stone. Remember Snow?"

He nodded.

"Whether Nylah is the one who brought it here or not, it won't matter once it's destroyed."

He tapped his thumb on his knee, his mind reeling with possibilities. "Does the witch's journal say how to activate the Thropynite's magic?"

Amber flipped through the images, scanning the

pages. "It only lists a spell to destroy it, but I'm sure Snow can help us with that too."

"How will we find their dimension?"

"We know the general area to look in, and now that we know *what* we're looking for, you can use your gift. I'd bet the bar you'll be able to feel a disturbance in the atmosphere where the entrance is."

He did sense a heaviness in the air when he was there with Cade and James, but he'd chalked it up to creep factor. Maybe he was sensing the entrance to the Grunch's dimension. "It's worth a shot."

"We can fix this." She scooted closer until her leg rested against his. "And we can be together."

He traced his fingers up her cheek, sliding them into her silky hair. There was still the issue that his wolf might not claim her, even if it fused with his soul, but he didn't mention it. For the first time since this ordeal began, he felt hope. No need to kill the mood.

"You're the only person I can imagine spending the rest of my life with," she said, "and I know... I know everything is going to work out. It has to. I love you, Noah."

His heart felt like it burst into a million pieces, swirled around in his chest, and stitched itself back together again. "I love you too."

She climbed into his lap, straddling his groin, and ran her hands up his bare chest to hook them behind his neck. Her fingers felt like silk against his skin. Leaning down, she brushed a tentative kiss to his lips.

"Should we be doing this in your parents' house?" he whispered.

Her only answer was to crush her mouth to his.

He held in his moan, the thought of what her father

might do if he found them together making him conscious of every sound they made. He almost stopped her, but as her lips glided down his neck, and she nipped his shoulder with her teeth, he said *screw it*. They were both consenting adults, for fuck's sake. They could do what they wanted.

He ran his hands up her sides to cup her breasts, and her nipples hardened beneath the satin as he teased them with his thumbs. Her lips parted on a deep inhale, her warm breath tickling his neck before she found his mouth once more. She tasted of mint, and as she slipped her tongue into his mouth to tangle with his, all the blood that was left in his head rushed to his groin.

He lifted her nightgown, tugging it upward until she raised her arms, allowing him to remove it and toss it aside. He slid his gaze down her form, taking in her delicate curves and smooth, lightly freckled skin before looking into her eyes. His mouth watered to taste her, and when she smiled, something snapped inside his chest like a glowstick coming to life. He still had no idea what his wolf was thinking, but the man needed her more than he needed air to breathe. He would die before he'd spend his life without her.

He stifled the growl rumbling in his chest and leaned forward, taking a nipple into his mouth while teasing the other with his thumb. She let out a breathy *ahh*, the seductive sound raising goosebumps on his skin.

Gliding his tongue upward between her breasts, he circled it around the dip in her collarbone before continuing his ascent to take her mouth in another kiss. How many times he had imagined this moment, he couldn't recall. But having her here, nearly naked in his arms, he felt complete.

Her hands roamed down his stomach, his muscles tightening as they found their way beneath the covers to grip his dick through his underwear. He shuddered, and she smiled, palming him, sliding her hand upward and back down beneath the fabric to grip his flesh.

An *mmm* resonated in his throat, and she rose to her knees, her gaze never leaving his as she pushed the sheets downward, exposing the rest of his body. Drawing her bottom lip between her teeth, she arched a brow and tugged off his boxer-briefs. She licked her lips as she gazed at his dick, and she took it in her hand once more, stroking it from base to tip, circling her finger around the sensitive head before stroking it again.

"Fuck, Amber. You're so goddamn sexy."

With a wicked grin, she lowered her head, taking him into her mouth. He moaned, closing his eyes and tipping his head back, reveling in the feel of the warm wetness enveloping him. She circled her tongue as she sucked him, and when she grazed her teeth over his tip, he nearly lost it.

"Come here." With his hand on the back of her head, he gently guided her toward his mouth. He kissed her, drinking her in and wrapping his arms around her.

"I need you, Noah." Her voice was a whisper against his lips.

"Then you'll have me." In one swift motion, he flipped her onto her back, and she gasped.

With his hips between her legs, he rubbed his cock against her, the thin strip of satin that separated them growing wet as he moved.

"Please, Noah." She nipped at his earlobe, sending shivers down his spine.

He kissed her neck, breathing in the intoxicating sweet

scent of her skin as he rocked his hips. God, he needed her. It took all his willpower to keep from ripping off her panties and taking her right that moment.

But he wanted to savor her. With the uncertainty of his condition, this could be the only moment he got to spend alone with her, and he intended to take his time and relish her body.

He worked his way downward, licking and kissing, caressing every inch of her delicate skin. She ran her hands over his back, gripping his shoulders and gasping as he grazed her nipple with his teeth. He took the other between his thumb and forefinger, and the soft moan emanating from her throat had to be the most beautiful sound he'd ever heard.

Amber was a goddess. Her scent, her sounds, her soul…everything about her called to him, enraptured him. He would do everything in his power to make her his mate, whether the pack approved of their union or not.

Resuming his descent, he glided his tongue down her stomach and pressed a kiss to her navel. Her hips moved beneath his chest, a silent plea for him to continue downward. He paused, resting his chin on her pelvis and gazing up at her. She was the most beautiful woman he'd ever seen.

"Please, Noah," she whispered, and he shuddered at her request. He wouldn't make her ask again.

Rising onto his knees, he slipped off her panties and settled his shoulders between her legs before gliding his tongue from slit to clit. She gasped, her entire body tensing, her hands fisting the sheets. The sweet taste of her made his head spin. He teased her sensitive nub with his tongue before gently sucking it between his lips.

He continued the rhythm, sucking and licking while

she writhed beneath him. When he slipped a finger inside, her breath came out in a rush. He could have stayed there all night. The knowledge that he could make her feel this much pleasure exhilarated him to no end, but as she whimpered, another whispered *please* escaped her lips. It was time to make her come.

Slipping a second finger inside her, he rotated his hand until he reached her sweet spot. As he bathed her clit in wet heat, he stroked her until her hips bucked and she gasped, biting her lip to keep from crying out.

He slowed his rhythm, bringing her down gently, and the tension in her body eased. Rising onto his elbows, he gazed at her, and she looked back at him with passion-drunk eyes.

"I need you inside me," she nearly growled. "Right now."

"Yes, ma'am." He crawled on top of her, filling her completely with one swift thrust.

She dropped her head back on the pillow and let out an erotic *mmm*.

Heaven help him, he could have come right then, but he wasn't ready for it to end. He pulled out, taking his dick in his hand and rubbing the head over her swollen clit. Teasing her, he slid halfway in, pulling out again and rubbing himself over her.

"You're driving me crazy," she whispered.

"That's the idea."

As he slid halfway in again, she grabbed his ass, pulling him toward her and lifting her hips until she took in his entire length. He couldn't hold back anymore. Slipping his arms beneath her shoulders, he held her tightly and pumped his hips.

She clung to him, wrapping her legs around his waist

to take him deeper and biting his shoulder as another orgasm made her entire body shudder. His own coiled in his core before rushing out in a release so intense it rocked him to his soul.

Collapsing on top of her, he hugged her tighter, nuzzling into her neck and making a silent vow that he would never let her go. As her breathing slowed, she relaxed her hold and turned her face toward him to kiss his forehead.

"I meant it when I said I love you." She kissed him again.

"So did I." He rolled onto his back and tugged her to his side.

She came to him, draping her leg across his hips and laying her head on his shoulder. As she traced her fingers across his chest, his eyes drifted shut, and he basked in the elated emotions swirling in his soul.

But a few minutes later, she sat up, breaking the trance he'd succumbed to. "We finally made it all the way without your wolf trying to eat me."

"Hmm." He laced his fingers behind his head. "I didn't feel him at all like I did before. I wonder why that is."

"I should go back to my room. We need to keep up the charade that we're not together." She rose from the bed and dressed.

Noah sat up and took her hand, bringing it to his lips. He was loath to let her go, but she was right. If this plan was going to work, they had to keep it all a secret. Even if it didn't work, he knew without a doubt he wanted to spend the rest of his life with her. He'd go rogue if that was what it took. "Listen, Amber. If, after we do this, my wolf doesn't claim you, I still…"

She slipped from his grasp and lowered her gaze.

Then he felt it. The wolf inside him rose to the surface, threatening to break free. He clenched his fists, willing the beast into submission. "We'll talk about it later. You should go."

Amber nodded and slipped out the door, taking his heart with her. As the latch clicked shut, his wolf relinquished, and Noah lay back, staring at the ceiling.

# CHAPTER SEVENTEEN

Amber tried to look sullen on the drive to New Orleans, putting on a show to convince her father she and Noah were over, but every time she caught Noah's gaze in the side mirror, her lips curved into a smile. Luckily, she was in the back seat, and her dad was focused on the road.

Making love to Noah had been better than she could have ever imagined. If she closed her eyes, she could still feel the contrast of his soft skin and hard muscles beneath her fingers, could still smell his woodsy scent and taste the salt of his skin.

Being with him had felt better than right. It had felt like fate. Now, if she could only convince his wolf to agree. Her heart began to sink at the thought, but she yanked it out of the depths before it could slip into despair. She had to focus on one thing at a time, lest she get caught in the vicious circle of *he loves me; his wolf loves me not.*

Noah loved her, and that was all that mattered for now. Maybe it was all that mattered period.

When they reached New Orleans, her dad dropped

Noah at his house first. Keeping up the act, he didn't look at her as he thanked her dad for the ride and climbed out of the truck. Amber crossed her arms, staring out the side window as her father turned toward her.

"Do you want to get in the front?" he asked.

"I'm fine here." At the moment, she fit the role of the teenager he treated her like, but she didn't dare chance blowing their cover. She could hardly contain her excitement as it was.

He sighed. "Suit yourself. I'll drop you by the bar so you can report what you learned in the archives to Luke." He backed out of the driveway and headed toward the French Quarter.

"There's no need. I doubt it's anything he doesn't already know," she lied. "I'll send him a text when I get home."

They rode in silence the rest of the way, and when her dad parked in her driveway, he turned around in his seat. "Amber, honey, you know I love you."

"I know. Thanks for the lift." She slid out of the truck and strode to her front porch. He was a fool to think he had a say in whom she chose as a mate. This wasn't the 1900s.

Inside, she closed her eyes and leaned her head against the door. The wood felt cool against her skin. "This is going to work," she whispered. If only she could make herself believe it.

She waited an hour to be certain her father was well on his way back to Jackson before heading out the door. Humid summer heat engulfed her as she strode onto the sidewalk and hung a right, heading toward Royal Street. Two- and three-story buildings dating back to the 1800s lined the streets. Shops and art galleries occupied the bottom floors, while wrought-iron balconies adorned with ferns and colorful potted flowers covered the second- and third-floor residential areas.

A saxophone player stood on the street corner playing a sad, slow tune, and Amber paused to listen. The music drifting on the air made her chest ache. New Orleans was her home, the Crescent City Wolf Pack her family, but Noah was her soulmate. She'd fought tooth and claw to insist no one but her could decide whom she took as a mate, but she would be taking that same choice away from Noah if she left him. If their plan worked and his wolf fused with his soul but didn't claim her, whether he waited for a fate-bound or not wasn't her decision. If he was willing to give up the chance to be with her, who was she to tell him no?

Her phone chimed with a text, and she stepped into the shade of a slate blue building to read the message. Her stomach fluttered when she saw it was from Noah: *I'm going to enlist help from Cade. He can keep a secret.*

She replied: *If you trust him, so do I. On my way to see Snow now.*

They were taking a risk involving other people, but based on what she'd read about the Grunch, they needed the help. She shuddered at the thought of her heart ending up on the gargoyle's dinner plate.

Her phone chimed again with another text from Noah: *Stay safe. I love you.*

She smiled as she keyed in her reply: *I love you too.* Damn, it felt good to type that.

Yes, they were risking their lives and their positions in the pack by attempting this without the alpha's permission. Hell, once her dad talked to his peers about Noah, they'd be going against the congress's ruling just by being in each other's presence. But seeing Noah's *I love you* put a spring in her step anyway.

She paused outside Spellbound Sweets, a witchy bakery, and peered through the window. Snow Connolly stood behind the counter, her platinum blonde hair glinting in the sunlight streaming through the glass. Her sister, Rain, owned the bakery, and she and Chase lived in the apartment upstairs. Amber took a deep breath, pushed open the door, and stepped inside.

The sweet scents of cinnamon and vanilla drifted on the air, and Snow slid a tray of frosted sugar cookies into a display case before looking up and beaming a smile. "Hey, Amber! What brings you in?"

She paced to the counter and drummed her fingers on the surface. "I need a favor. Is Rain around?"

"She's out running errands. She should be back in a few hours if you want to check in later."

Amber peered at the magical cookies beneath the glass. The witches sold them as "spells" with a wink and a nod for the humans. The "love spell" was heart-shaped and frosted red, while the "money spell" was a dollar sign frosted green. In reality, they all contained the same magic: a clarity spell to help the consumer focus on their true goals.

Amber didn't need a spell to know her true goals. She had to save Nylah and make Noah her mate...no matter the cost. "Actually, I'm here to see you. I need a potion."

Snow wiped her hands on a dishtowel and closed the display case. "Well, you've come to the right place. What can I whip up for you?"

Amber glanced behind her to be sure no one had entered the shop. "This is a covert operation. If anyone in the pack finds out what I'm doing, I'll be in shit so deep, I'll never dig my way out. Can you keep a secret?"

Snow arched a brow. "Are you kidding? I'm the queen of keeping secrets. Just ask Rain."

"This is what I need." She opened the photo of the spell she'd found in the witch's journal and offered Snow her phone.

Her eyes widened as she scanned the page, and she let out a low whistle. "That's some potent stuff. What are you going to do with it?"

"Noah and I are going to rescue Nylah and put an end to the Grunch."

Snow motioned for Amber to follow her into the kitchen. "Why can't the pack know? Sounds like it should be an *all hands on deck* mission."

Amber stepped around the counter and strode into the kitchen. "Because Noah is the reason the Grunch were awakened in the first place." She explained the situation as Snow pulled various herbs and liquids from the shelves and set them on the counter next to a copper bowl.

"Nylah brought the Thropynite here to force Noah's wolf to awaken," Snow mused, "but instead, she woke up the Grunch?"

"Exactly."

"Damn, girl. That is some deep shit."

"Tell me about it." She leaned against the counter, crossing her legs at the ankles. "But if we can pull this off, no one will ever have to know."

"Let me see the spell again. I think it continues on the next page." Snow held out her hand, and Amber gave her the phone. Pinching the screen, she zoomed in on the ingredients list and nodded. "Elderflower. Got it. Eye of newt. Got it. Did you know that's just mustard seed?"

"I had no idea." Amber peered over her shoulder at the phone.

Snow flipped to the next image. "Oh, wait." She zoomed the screen. "Damn. This isn't just potent magic; it's deadly."

"What is it?" Amber took the phone when Snow handed it to her.

"It calls for wolfsbane-infused DUME oil."

Amber's stomach sank. Wolfsbane was a highly toxic herb that could kill a shifter in under an hour. Supposedly death by wolfsbane was an excruciating way to go, and it was used as a supernatural lethal injection for more than a century. The congress finally ruled it a cruel and unusual punishment, making it illegal for any werewolf, shifter or not, to possess it.

"I'm familiar with wolfsbane, but what is DUME oil?"

"It stands for 'Death Unto My Enemies.' It's Hoodoo black magic."

"Oh, hell." Amber shoved her phone into her pocket. "I don't suppose you know how to get ahold of some, do you?"

Snow took a deep breath and slowly shook her head. "A Vodouisant would be more familiar with Hoodoo than a witch. Why don't you ask Odette?"

"For the same reason I don't want Rain to know what I'm doing. She'd feel obligated to tell her mate, and we can't let anyone find out how the Thropynite got here."

"Gotcha. Your secret is safe with me, but I—" The door chimed, signaling someone had entered the bakery.

"I'm back, Snow. You can take a break now," Rain's voice drifted on the air.

"Crap. She's early." Snow ushered Amber to the back door. "If you can get your hands on the DUME oil, I'm happy to whip up the potion for you. I normally don't mess with black magic, but if I can think of someone who might know where to find some, I'll let you know."

"Thank you." Amber slipped out the back door and made her way up the alley to the street, hanging a right and striding away from the shop before dialing Noah's number. He didn't answer, so she hung up without leaving a message. He wouldn't know where to get wolfsbane-infused DUME oil any more than she would.

"Think, Amber. Think." Her determined strides carried her through the French Quarter like a woman on a mission, though where she was headed, she had no clue. She paced up one street and down another, racking her brain for a solution to this problem. Not only did she need to find and bargain with a black magic practitioner, but she had to get a tincture containing wolfsbane. How many supernatural laws could she break in a single act of defiance?

While the pack had been on good terms with the Voodoo folks for decades, they didn't get involved with Hoodoo practitioners. Those guys were always up to no good, using and abusing the magic for their own self-gain. Hoodoo was like Voodoo, but without the religious or moral compass for guidance.

After half an hour of wandering, Amber found herself on Dumaine, across the street from Odette's House of Voodoo, and she paused on the sidewalk, staring at the dark green wooden door. If anyone would know a Hoodoo practitioner who might help her, it would be Odette.

But she couldn't ask her. She might as well go straight to Luke and tell him everything if she was going to get a shifter's mate involved. She could always slip in and ask one of the other Vodouisants inside for help. But if word got back to Odette, their plan would fall apart faster than a strand of cheap Mardi Gras beads smacking the pavement. She needed to find someone familiar with Hoodoo whom Odette never spoke to.

*Of course!* She mentally smacked herself upside the head for not thinking of him sooner. Odette's cousin Emile was a *traiteur*—a Voodoo faith healer—who lived out in the swamps. They had a sordid history and never spoke to each other, which made him the perfect person to ask for help locating a Hoodoo practitioner.

A quick internet search provided Emile's number, and she sat on a bench in the shade of a tree in Jackson Square to make the call. While the existence of werewolves was kept a secret from the humans, talk of Hoodoo, Voodoo, and witchcraft was so common in New Orleans, no one would bat an eye at the conversation she was about to have.

A warm breeze caressed her sweat-slicked skin, providing a welcome relief from the sauna of the French Quarter, and she gazed up at the massive statue of Andrew Jackson sitting atop a horse in the center of the Square.

A little girl squealed with delight as she ran by, her brother hot on her heels with a bubble gun, and Amber's chest gave a squeeze. If they could make this plan work, she and Noah might bring their own children to the park one day. Wouldn't it be something if they had twins?

She shook her head, chasing away the daydream, and dialed Emile's number. When he answered, she inhaled deeply before speaking. "Hi, Emile. My name is Amber Mason, and I'm with the Crescent City Wolf Pack. I'm looking for a Hoodoo practitioner who might sell me some DUME oil, and I wondered if you might know of someone who could help."

Silence hung heavy on the other end of the line, and it lasted so long she nearly thought the call had dropped.

"Did Odette tell you to call? What is she getting on about?" Irritation laced his voice.

Amber clutched the phone tighter. "No. No, she doesn't know anything about this."

"Well, I'm sure she can help you with whatever you need."

"Wait! Please don't hang up." She paused, hoping against hope he was still on the line. When she heard a heavy sigh, she continued, "I'm in trouble, and no one in my pack can find out about it. Please, I just need the name of a Hoodoo practitioner, and then I'll leave you alone."

"DUME oil isn't to be played with."

"Believe me, if it wasn't a life-or-death situation, I wouldn't mess with it. I'll be careful." Her knee bounced, shaking the bench, so she rested her hand on her thigh to still her fidgeting. What would her packmates say if they knew what she was up to? Most likely that she'd gone insane. The shifters would want to attack the Grunch, using brute force to vanquish them, despite the fact they'd tried and failed already.

Yes, Amber's plan was dangerous, but far less so than anything the "men in charge" would come up with. A full-frontal attack against who-knew-how-many Grunch would result in too many casualties. Destroying the Thropynite was the best course of action, even if she had to break a few laws to accomplish it.

"You didn't get this information from me." Emile gave her a name and address, which she scribbled onto the back of a business card.

"Thank you. If you happen to speak to Odette…"

"I won't. Good day." The line went dead.

"Well, okay then." She rose to her feet and typed the address into her phone. "Jeez, that's in Algiers. He didn't know a Hoodoo man in the Quarter?" At least she didn't have to trek into the swamp to find him.

She headed to her house and climbed into her Mazda, turning the AC on full blast before pulling onto the road. Traffic was light over the Crescent City Connection Bridge, the muddy Mississippi stretching out beneath her, and her pulse thrummed as she exited onto General De Gaulle Drive. Her hands went slick with sweat, and she wiped her palms on her jeans at a traffic light.

Was she insane for doing this? Her entire life, she'd stood in the shadow of her brother. A second-born in the alpha line didn't get much attention when her power was passive. Any time she ran into trouble, Luke took care of it. He was a good brother and a good alpha, but damn it, it was her turn to shine. Noah and Nylah were *her* best friends, and she should be the one to save them.

She had a duty to the pack, and Noah was the only man who could help her fulfill it. She had to make him her mate. Besides, it wasn't like Luke or the others never broke any laws for their mates. Amber would do what had to be done. End of story.

"This can't be right." She stopped in the parking lot of a convenience store and checked the address Emile gave her. "The Hoodoo man sells his spells out of a Stop-N-Save?" She killed the engine and climbed out of the car, clutching her purse strap on her shoulder as she entered the store.

Three rows of shelves stood in the center of the space, and refrigerated cases lined two of the walls. A cashier stood behind a plexiglass-encased checkout counter, and as Amber cast her gaze in his direction, he didn't look up from his phone. To the eye, the shop looked like any other convenience store.

Her nose told a different story. While her olfactory senses weren't nearly as powerful as a shifter's, she did have a good sense of smell. The sharp scent of ginger mingled with the sweet aroma of calamus root…not your typical Stop-N-Save bouquet.

She spotted a set of black beaded curtains hanging in a doorway at the back of the shop. The cashier still hadn't acknowledged her presence, so she moseyed back, pretending to look at the candies on the shelf as she moved.

After wiping her clammy hands on her pants once more, she pulled the curtain aside and stepped through the doorway. A shelf with jars of herbs and bottles of who-knew-what stood to her right, and a mobile made of animal bones hung in the center of the room.

"Hello?" Her voice sounded tiny, so she cleared her throat and tried again. "Hello? I'm looking for Papa Fortune." Now she sounded like the confident woman she was.

She reached a hand toward a jar containing a clear liquid and what looked like a body part—was that a human ear?—but she stopped before she could touch it. The last thing she needed was to accidentally curse herself.

"Is anyone here?" She walked deeper into the room.

A set of dried animal hides hung from a line attached to the back wall. She recognized the furs of raccoon, nutria, rabbit, and opossum, but there were a few she couldn't place. Beneath the hides, the poor creatures' severed feet dangled like ornaments.

"What do you need, child?" An old man with weathered skin and milky eyes shuffled through another door. He stopped in front of her and held out his hands, palms up, before making a come-here gesture with his fingers.

Amber placed her hands on top of his, and he clutched them, his grip incredibly strong for someone his age. She tried to pull away, but he held on tighter, closing his eyes and nodding. His magic vibrated on her skin, sharp and strong. When he finally released her, she fought the urge to wipe her hands on her pants.

"I don't get many werewolf visitors." He hobbled behind a wooden counter and slid onto a stool. "What can I do for you?"

She swallowed the lump that had formed in her throat, glancing at the dead animals. Thankfully, he hadn't displayed any wolf hides. "I need a tincture of wolfsbane-infused DUME oil."

His eyes widened briefly. "What do you need it for?"

"I'd rather not say."

"No, I guess you wouldn't." He crossed his arms. "DUME oil ain't cheap, child. Powerful magic always has a high price."

"How much?" She had a healthy savings account she could dip into. She'd spend it all if she had to. Anything to help her friends.

His laugh turned into a wet cough, and she curled her lip, leaning away as he hacked. "Money can't buy DUME oil." He coughed again like he was hacking up something nasty.

She stepped back and gave him the side-eye. It figured he'd require something other than cash. "What do you want then?"

"Nothing you have, but you know someone who has it."

Amber tensed, and her nails cut into her palms as she clenched her fists. They were running out of time. This guy needed to stop the cryptic bullshit and tell her what he wanted.

"Name your price," she hissed through clenched teeth.

Evil sparked in his cloudy brown eyes, his smile looking more like a grimace. "Shifter blood." He raised his brows and leaned back against the wall, watching her as he awaited her reaction.

All the blood drained from Amber's head and pooled in her stomach, churning in a nauseating swirl of defeat. Not only was it against pack law for shifters to give their blood to anyone, but it was a crime punishable by death. "You know that's impossible."

"Do I? If you need the DUME oil that bad, you'll pay the price." He slid off his stool and shuffled toward his shelves, all but dismissing her.

Shifter blood was powerful, and it had the potential to be used in all sorts of black magic spells. Spells that should never be cast. There was no way in hell any of the shifters in her pack would willingly donate their blood because the consequences would be worse than losing Nylah to the Grunch. A practitioner could rain death and destruction on the entire city with a few drops.

Papa Fortune didn't seem like a man who would be easy to fool, but she had to try something. "If I bring you the blood, you'll give me the oil?"

He laughed and then cleared his throat. "Oh no. You bring the shifter to me. One shifter. Don't bring no more. Once I see him shift, we'll do a bloodletting, and then you can have the oil."

"Is there any other way?" she asked.

"That's my price. Take it or leave it, but I doubt you'll find anybody else willing to give a werewolf DUME oil."

Amber turned on her heel and stalked out of the store. They were out of options. The only way to defeat the Grunch would be to bring in the entire pack, and if they did that, she'd never see Noah or Nylah again.

She climbed into her car and clutched the steering wheel in a death grip, squeezing until her knuckles turned white. Even if she could find a shifter willing to give her blood, she could never let a Hoodoo man get his hands on it.

They were screwed.

## CHAPTER EIGHTEEN

Alrick glared at the she-wolf as she slept in her prison, and he contemplated his next move. His loneliness had allowed her to live for this long, but his agitation with her insubordination was beginning to outweigh his need for company.

As he watched her eyes move back and forth beneath her lids, he realized somewhere deep inside him, a tiny bud of hope had bloomed. She knew what he was. She could look at his disfigured form and not laugh…not cower in fear.

Against his will, his humanity had leaked toward the surface, his human heart somehow making room for this magical being, this insult to nature.

A growl rumbled in his chest, his anger seething like poison, seeping into the cracks and dissolving the unwelcome emotion that had tried to blossom. He was a fool to allow such unfounded hope to invade his psyche, like he'd been a fool to believe his witch could love such an abomination as himself.

He was designed to kill. When the Sect recruited him,

he'd vowed to give up all relationships with anyone but his kind. These damned emotions were nothing more than a burden. A weakness he'd given in to twice. What would his brothers think if they awoke now? They'd probably tear him limb from limb for bringing another female into their realm, and he would deserve it.

He narrowed his eyes as she rolled onto her side. How dare she entrance him? He had the power to glean all the information he'd tried to coax from her lips with a simple piercing of her skull, yet she'd convinced him to let her live, in spite of her defiance.

With a grunt, he passed through the prison wall and wrapped his talons around her throat. Her lids flew open when he squeezed, and as he lifted her from the bed, she scratched at his hands, her feet flailing in the air.

"Please." Her voice was a wisp of air from her lips, but he was finished showing the she-wolf mercy.

He swung his arm, releasing his grip and hurling her against the wall. Her head hit the invisible surface with a satisfying *thwack*, and she slid to the floor, landing in a heap. She groaned, and he kicked her. The sound of her ribs snapping didn't give him nearly enough pleasure.

It was time for the she-wolf to die, but first, he'd make her suffer. He would kill every member of her pack one by one, and he would start with her brother. Forget the cover of darkness. The entire city would soon cower at the sight of him.

---

Noah bit into an alligator sausage hot dog and gazed out over Frenchman Street as a five-piece band played a jazzy tune for the tourists milling about in the summer heat.

Cade sat across from him at their wooden table on the second-floor gallery, silently sipping his soda as he mulled over what Noah had said.

A dollop of the crawfish étouffée topping plopped onto Noah's plate as he finished the last bite, and he scooped it up with his finger, savoring the last bit of what could be his final meal.

"Damn, man. That's heavy," Cade finally said. "I'm down for a clandestine operation, but are you sure you don't want to get the pack involved? These guys have ripped out the hearts of seven people now, and we don't know how many we'll be up against."

"Rescuing Nylah will be for nothing if she's thrown in the pit for the rest of her life."

Cade took a bite of his Polish sausage and chewed slowly, swallowing before he spoke, "We'll both be joining her if this goes south."

A woman screamed, drawing their attention to the street below, where a bachelorette party was getting an early start. One of the women had tripped over the curb, breaking her stiletto and landing flat on her ass. Her friends hauled her up, and she pulled a pair of flip-flops from her purse before slipping them on and continuing down the sidewalk.

"Six months ago, our only worry would have been which woman in that group we'd be taking home," Cade said. "Now we could be facing jail time, or worse."

"We'll have to make sure we don't screw it up. I can hold the bastard. I've done it before."

"True, but he still got away."

"Because I let go. I thought y'all had it under control, but I'll hold on to the end this time. You and Nylah can take them out while I hold them still."

Cade blew out a slow breath and lowered his gaze.

"She's alive. I can feel she is, and Amber can too." His chest warmed at the mention of her name. "We can do this."

His friend nodded. "I'm in."

After clearing their table, they made their way downstairs and out onto Frenchman Street. Jazz music drifted out from the clubs as they strolled to the intersection and hung a right, away from the busy area.

"When is this going down?" Cade asked.

Noah followed him across the street, into the shade of the massive oak trees lining the neutral ground dividing the road. "As soon as possible. Amber's getting the potion to destroy the Thropynite, so as soon as I hear from her, we'll head out to Grunch Road."

"Are you sure that's where the pocket dimension is?"

"The energy felt different when we scouted the area before. It was heavy, like something was disturbing the natural flow. I didn't know what I was looking for at the time, but now that I do, it makes sense."

"Sounds like a plan." A mischievous grin lighted on Cade's lips. "Do you want to go for an afternoon hunt while you wait for your woman?"

Noah huffed. "I'm not allowed to shift without an alpha present."

He raised his brows. "You're also not allowed to hunt demons or see Amber, both of which you're about to do."

Noah stopped walking and squinted, looking more inward than at anything in front of him. "True."

"It'll be good to get some practice in…just in case you can't hold them with your magic. If the Grunch are as badass as the legends say, we'll need all the wolfpower we can get."

He shouldn't. He was already skating on thin ice with both the pack and the national congress. One slip-up, and he could face life in the pit…or worse. He gazed up at the cloudless sky, letting the sun warm his face. *Screw it.* That was exactly where he'd be headed if their plan didn't work. Why be cautious now? "I'll drive."

They rode in silence on the ten-mile drive to the hunting grounds, which was fine with Noah. Cade was right; he did need to practice shifting without an alpha around before they took on the Grunch. That didn't mean he wasn't scared shitless, though. Who knew what his wolf would do with no form of authority to guide him. He was about to find out.

He parked behind a tree alongside the road, and they trekked deep into the swampy area before shifting. His wolf came to the surface without hesitation, as usual. Turning from man to beast never was his problem. He expected his wolf to challenge Cade like he had the alpha, but instead, he hunted alongside his friend like their wolves were old pals.

For a moment, he let go of all his worries, and just let his wolf run. He didn't try to exert dominance over the beast, didn't concern himself with whether or not he'd be able to return to his human form. He simply enjoyed the ride, and damn, was it exhilarating.

Until the faintest hint of sulfur and rotting garbage reached his senses. Cade skidded to a stop, his nose in the air, and Noah hoped to Hades his wolf's inborn instinct to hunt demons would kick in. Lucky for him, his beast stopped too, a ridge of fur standing on end down the middle of his back. A fiend was near.

A branch broke to their right, and Noah's wolf swung his head in the direction of the disturbance. Cade growled, flattening his ears against his head, the sound making Noah's skin prick. They stood side by side, crouching low as the demon emerged from the trees.

Noah's growl intensified. This was no ordinary demon; it was the same gargoyle-like fiend the pack had attacked before.

"Where is the she-wolf's brother?" He lifted his head and sniffed the air. "I can smell his presence."

The fiend *did* have Nylah. Noah reached out to his wolf, trying to regain control so he could face the Grunch, but the animal refused to relent.

Cade cut his eyes toward Noah, appearing to speak with his thoughts, but Noah's lack of connection to his beast made it impossible for the man to understand. Whatever Cade was planning, his wolf didn't care.

He lunged, snapping his jaws at the creature and sinking his teeth into a patch of soft flesh on its side. The demon roared and grabbed Noah by the scruff of his neck before hurling him into the bayou.

Muddy water engulfed him. He tried again to shift to his human form, but the shock made his wolf hold on tighter. He paddled, breaking the surface and then swimming toward the bank.

"Stand down, and I'll let you live," the demon growled. "Tell the she-wolf's brother Alrick is coming for him. His heart will be my next meal."

If Noah were in control, he'd have growled. This was the same demon who held the witch captive a century ago.

Cade inched toward Alrick, and the demon backed up until he stood on the water's edge. Noah's wolf locked his gaze on the fleshy area of his ankle. With his paws digging into the muddy bank, he hauled himself up and latched on to Alrick's leg before yanking with all his might.

The demon slipped in the mud and tumbled backward. His size and the weight of his stone-like flesh caused him to sink, and Noah's wolf scrambled onto the bank before shaking out his fur.

Alrick bobbed to the surface, his arms flailing. "Help! I can't swim." His voice had changed, sounding more like a man than a fiend. The wolves stood there watching him struggle. Noah would have preferred to drag him from the water and tear him to pieces, but for once, his wolf made the right decision and let the bayou be his end.

There were only two ways to kill a pure demon: pierce the heart or cut off its head. Even then, the fiend wouldn't die. It would simply be banished back to the hell from where it came.

Alrick was half-demon. Not even that. The fiend in him had been magically fused with his soul, and it seemed his human side could succumb to drowning. *Good riddance.*

After sinking again, he struggled to the surface and gasped before he spoke, "You're next." Then, in a flash of magic, he disappeared.

Noah's wolf shook out his fur again, sending muddy water in every direction before releasing his hold. He shifted to human and ran a hand through his sopping wet hair.

Cade shifted and clapped a hand on his shoulder. "That was amazing, man. Much better than my plan. Next time, clue me in, though."

"I would if I could." He shook his head. "He's got Nylah. We need to find him *now*."

"Slow down. Your battleplan was pretty detailed, and it didn't involve busting in with our teeth bared. Without the potion that destroys the Thropynite, our friend Alrick seems indestructible."

Noah ground his teeth. "We can't even drown the bastard with the way he teleports. That's one strong-ass demon inside him."

"Tell me about it. He's even out in the daylight. I've never seen a fiend escape a battle with four werewolves. We can't beat him with three unless we can get our hands on that stone."

"You're right. Let's swing by my place for some dry clothes, and…" He tugged his phone from his pocket. Thankfully, it had been absorbed by the magic when he was in wolf form and was still in working order. "Amber called three times. She left a voicemail."

He hit the speaker button and played the message: *We've got a big problem. Meet me at Spellbound Sweets as soon as you can.*

"Uh oh." Cade jerked his head toward the truck. "What do you think the problem is?"

Noah paced by his side and climbed into the driver's seat. "She was working on the potion with Snow. We better get there fast."

They swung by Noah's place so he could rinse off the swamp muck and change his clothes, and then they headed straight to the witches' bakery. A bell chimed when he opened the door, and a dozen different sugary scents blasted his nostrils.

Snow appeared in the doorway leading to the kitchen, and she gestured to the entrance. "Lock it, will you? And come on back."

Noah twisted the deadbolt before he and Cade stepped around the counter and followed her into the kitchen area.

Amber ran to him, throwing her arms around him and squeezing tightly.

"What's going on?" Noah kissed the top of her head before leaning back to look at her. "You said we have a problem?"

"We do." She stepped out of his embrace. "But I think I have a plan. Oh, Snow, this is Cade. Have y'all met?"

Snow grinned and offered him her hand. "No, we have not. It's a pleasure."

A faint shade of pink tinted Cade's cheeks. "The pleasure is mine."

Amber pressed her lips together and gave Noah a funny look. Yep, his friend was smitten.

"Snow can't make the potion without DUME oil," Amber said, "and we can only get that from a Hoodoo practitioner."

"Do you need us to help you locate one?" Cade asked Snow.

"I found one," Amber said. "I also paid him a visit, and that's where the problem lies."

Snow winked at Cade before turning around and taking a copper bowl from a shelf. Noah elbowed his friend in the ribs, trying to get him to focus on the problem at hand.

Amber ran her hands down her face, pressing them against her lips before lifting them and dropping them at her sides. "He wants shifter blood, and he won't accept any other payment."

Noah's stomach sank. "That's…" He was about to say "impossible," but at this point, was it really? He chewed the inside of his cheek, pondering whether he was willing to commit a crime punishable by death.

"That's what he wants from you," Cade said. "But

what if someone who wasn't a werewolf tried to get some? Surely he'd ask for a different form of payment."

"We tried." Amber leaned her hip against a counter. "Snow went, and he wanted her to sacrifice her first-born child."

"That bastard." Cade's brow slammed down over his eyes.

"Black magic isn't cheap," Snow said.

Noah rubbed his forehead. "You said you had a plan. I've heard rumors about the things that can be done with shifter blood, and I don't want to be the cause of more death." He'd already caused enough.

"Hear me out," Amber said. "I believe, since your wolf hasn't fused with your soul, that your blood won't have the shifter magical qualities if it's taken while you're in human form."

"I don't…" He pressed his lips together, his mind reeling at the idea. It was possible. Much like he was a detached soul along for the ride when his wolf had control, the beast felt like a foreign body inside him when the man was in control. Her plan could work, but… "There's no way to know that for sure."

"I can test it." Snow held a small copper bowl in one hand, a scalpel in the other.

His nostrils flared as he blew out a long, slow breath. If he agreed to this, he'd be committing the crime twice, giving his blood to both a witch and a Hoodoo man. Even if Luke wanted to go easy on him, the alpha would have no choice but to enact the swiftest punishment.

"I know it's a big ask." Amber rested her hand on his arm. "So if you don't want to, we'll figure out another way."

He shook his head. His sister's life was on the line. "There is no other way." He gave Cade a hard look.

"I'm in this, man," his friend said. "Whatever it takes."

Noah nodded and clapped him on the shoulder before looking at Snow.

"Your secret is safe with me." Snow drew an X over her heart.

"Let's do this." He took the scalpel from Snow's hand. "How much do you need?"

"One drop will do it. This is a potion witches use to test the potency of an ingredient before using it in a spell. I enchanted it to look for shifter magic, so if your human blood has the wolf gene in it, black speckles will form on the surface like someone sprinkled it with pepper."

Noah eyed the potion. At least he didn't have to drink it this time. "That's all it will do? It can't be used for anything else?"

Snow shook her head and gestured to a bottle of pink liquid. "It won't, but I'll pour a neutralizer into it and dump it down the sink as soon as we're done."

"You can trust her." Amber squeezed his arm.

Sucking in a deep breath, he jabbed the scalpel into the tip of his finger. Blood pooled on his skin, and he turned his hand over, allowing it to drip into the bowl. He pressed his thumb against the wound to stop the bleeding as Snow swirled the contents of the bowl.

She set it on the counter, and they all gathered around, watching the lemon-yellow liquid as it bubbled and hissed. Amber slid her arm around his waist, reminding him to breathe. The concoction settled, and Snow swiped a spoon through it.

"Nothing." She stirred it in a circle. "The potion is clear."

Noah stepped toward the bowl and stared at it intently, looking for any speck of black that the witch might have missed. He found nothing. A sense of relief mixed with the anxiety churning in his core. They were one step closer to rescuing Nylah. "What do we do if he uses this test?"

"We'll have to make sure the transaction is complete before he does," Amber said.

Snow held up a small burlap bag. "This is binding powder. It solidifies any contract made. Be sure to seal the deal before you give him the blood. Amber knows how to use it."

"Y'all have thought of everything, haven't you?"

"We talked through all the scenarios and the possible outcomes," she said. "And we found solutions for everything that could go wrong."

Noah kissed Amber on the cheek. Her sharp mind was one of the things he loved about her. "How much does the Hoodoo man want? More than a drop, I'm sure." He looked at Snow. "Do you have a bottle?"

Amber cleared her throat. "He didn't say. I'm supposed to bring you, and only you, to his shop. He wants to see you shift and witness the blood draw."

His heart sank. That was a whole other problem he *knew* she didn't have a solution for.

# CHAPTER NINETEEN

Amber squeezed Noah's hand across the console in the Hoodoo shop's parking lot. His posture was relaxed, his expression stoic, making him seem much calmer than she felt. "It's very brave of you to do this."

He laughed cynically. "Maybe. Or maybe it's downright stupid. Should we count how many laws we're breaking?"

"I'd rather not."

He turned in the passenger seat to face her. "You're the one who's brave. You found this guy and came here all on your own, having no idea what you'd encounter inside."

She lifted one shoulder. "I'll do anything for you and Nylah."

"I love you, Amber. You have no idea how much I respect and admire you."

Her heart warmed at his words. She did have an idea. He was willing to give up his chance at finding a fatebound to be with her, and that told her all she needed to know. "I love you too."

"I don't want you anywhere near me when I shift in

there. I don't know how my wolf will react to Papa Fortune, but I do know how he reacts to you."

She rested her hand against his cheek. "I'll be careful."

Her pulse thrummed as they entered the convenience store that fronted for the Hoodoo shop. This time, the cashier looked up from his post at the register, his eyes widening as his gaze locked on Noah.

Amber ignored the man and took Noah's hand, leading him through the beaded curtain. He cringed as they stepped inside, his nose wrinkling, no doubt in response to the pungent odors of the Hoodoo man's concoctions.

"Papa Fortune?" she called, her voice sounding much more confident than she actually was. "I brought the payment you asked for."

The old man shuffled in from a back room, his gaze skeptical as he glared at them. "You found a shifter willing to give his blood awful quick. Ain't it a crime in your pack? One punishable by death?"

She stiffened at the delight behind his words. "I can be very persuasive."

"I bet you can. Come." He held his hands toward Noah. "Let me read you to be certain you're a shifter."

Icy dread flushed through Amber's veins. She had no idea the kind of magic Papa Fortune possessed. What if he could tell Noah's wolf wasn't fused? If he figured out their trick, he could curse them both.

She stepped in front of Noah. "You said you wanted to see him shift. Isn't that proof enough?"

He narrowed his eyes at her. "Yes, I suppose it is. Follow me."

The old man led them through a doorway into a small room with dirty beige walls and scuffed linoleum. It smelled of mold and death, and her body shuddered as she entered the space. A large window with thick glass occupied most of the far wall, and a narrow doorway with six deadbolts stood to its right.

"What is this?" Amber padded to the window and peered into the next room. A heavy wooden table about seven feet long stood in the center of the room. A counter lined the left wall, and next to the array of herbs and potions sat a…was that a shriveled-up rat? She shuddered again.

"I'm not asking you any questions, child." Papa Fortune unlocked the deadbolts and opened the door. "I expect the same respect."

Noah stood next to her, and nervous energy rolled off him in waves. "I assume you want me to go in there to shift?"

"Can't have you attacking me now, can I?" Papa Fortune gestured for Noah to enter the room.

"I'll be right out here." Amber filled her voice with as much reassurance as she could muster…which wasn't much. She didn't want to be left out here with Papa Fortune any more than she wanted Noah to be trapped in there with the dead rat.

Noah stepped through the door, and the Hoodoo man locked all six deadbolts. Amber watched Noah through the glass, giving him a nod of encouragement and trying her best not to look worried. She crossed her fingers and said a silent prayer to whatever gods might be listening for him to have control of his wolf.

His body shimmered, and he transformed quickly. As his gaze locked on Papa Fortune, he bared his teeth, letting out a rumbling growl. Amber stepped out of the wolf's view so she wouldn't aggravate the situation more. She could only imagine the beast was having flashbacks to the examination room at the congress's headquarters.

Papa Fortune drummed his fingers together and laughed. "This is the first time a werewolf has graced me with a request. I thank you, child."

Amber slid her hand into her pocket and gripped the bag of binding dust. "There's your proof. Let him return to human so we can seal this deal."

"Not so fast." He turned to a shelving unit and picked up a small knife before shoving the handle toward her. She took it out of instinct, and then he offered her a glass bottle.

"What…?" She didn't need to finish her question. He wanted *her* to perform the bloodletting, and as he unlocked the deadbolts, she realized he wanted her to do it while Noah was in wolf form. *Oh, shit.*

"Fill the bottle, and the DUME oil is yours."

"Are you crazy? You want me to try to cut a werewolf?" Panic laced her voice, and it was no mystery why. Not only would Noah's wolf most likely maim her if she went anywhere near him, but they had only tested his blood while in human form. Drawing the blood from his wolf would give the Hoodoo man access to magic no one should have.

"I ain't about to put myself in danger. You want the oil, you'll get in there and get the blood." He swung open the door, grabbed Amber by the arm, and shoved her inside.

Her heart lodged in her throat, and she spun toward the door, gripping the knob with one hand and slamming her shoulder against the thick wood. At the sound of the locks sliding into place, ice flushed through her veins.

Clutching both the bottle and the knife in her left

hand, she slowly turned around to face the wolf, and he crouched, his lips peeling back to reveal his massive canines. He growled, and she pressed her back against the door.

"I love you." Her voice was barely a whisper, so she cleared her throat and tried again. "I love you."

His posture began to relax, his growl softening.

"I love both of you—the man and the wolf—no matter how you feel about me."

The growl turned into a whimper, and the wolf lay on his belly. Amber's breath came out in a rush. It seemed Noah had control…for now.

*Think, Amber. Think.* She looked at the small blade in her hand and then at the wolf lying on the concrete floor. An idea formed in her mind, and she pushed from the door, taking a tentative step toward him.

"I need you to lie still, okay? Noah, can you give me a sign that you're in control?" She took another step. The wolf studied her curiously.

"I'm going to assume that you are." She looked through the window, where Papa Fortune watched her with anticipation in his eyes. Positioning herself between the wolf and the window, she dropped to her knees and lowered her voice. "Don't move."

Her hand trembled as she scooted closer. The wolf narrowed his eyes. "I love you. I'm not going to hurt you."

She glanced over her shoulder before jabbing the tip of the knife into the concrete next to Noah's leg. The wolf flinched, jerking away from the blade, and she made a *shushing* sound, reaching toward him to calm the beast. "It's okay," she whispered. "I love you, remember? One more time."

Raising the knife above her head, she slammed it

down again, grazing the fur on his shoulder as she jabbed it into the floor. The tip snapped off, lodging in the concrete, and the wolf yelped and jumped to his feet.

"It won't work." She rose, turning to the window. "His hide is too tough in this form. We'll have to do it while he's human."

Amber moved toward the door, and the wolf growled. "Let me out, please." She banged on the wood.

The wolf flattened his ears against his head and bared his teeth. Amber sucked in a shaky breath, her pulse humming in her ears as she knocked again. "You need to let me out so he can shift."

She turned to the wolf and straightened her spine. The beast had been fine in her presence a moment ago. Why was he growling now? All she wanted to do was leave the damn room. "You are supposed to be my mate. You can't be treating me this way."

He pricked one ear, and then the other. Amber gripped the doorknob, counting the locks as they unlatched. *One…two…* Her words had subdued the wolf, but she had no idea how long it would last. *Three… four… five… Come on, old man.* As the sixth lock disengaged, she threw open the door, rushing out of the room and slamming it behind her. "What took you so long?"

The Hoodoo man cut his gaze between her and the wolf in the next room. "I thought werewolves could shift on command. Why hasn't he turned human yet?"

Amber gazed through the window. The animal's expression was strained; he was fighting the shift. "His wolf is very powerful. Once it comes to the surface, it takes time for the man to regain control."

Papa Fortune took the knife from her hand and gazed at the broken tip. "That's one hell of a hide."

She pressed her hand against the glass. "Noah, it's time to come back to me. We've got things to do, remember?"

It took a few minutes, but Noah finally returned to his human form, and Amber opened the door. He looked at her in awe. "How did you…?"

"We'll talk about it later," she whispered. Honestly, she had no idea how she got so close to his wolf without being mauled, other than he had finally figured out she was a friend.

Papa Fortune's shoes scuffled on the floor as he entered the room and handed Noah a new blade. "Fill the bottle."

Amber retrieved it from the floor and set it on the table. Noah sliced the side of his palm, letting blood drip into the open container. When it reached the top, Amber corked it and swept it from the surface before the Hoodoo man could grab it.

"I'll handle the rest." She clutched the bottle of Noah's blood tightly, while he pressed a rag to his hand. Hopefully Papa Fortune wouldn't notice Noah didn't heal as quickly as a shifter should. Any suspicion from him could negate this deal.

When Noah furrowed his brow, she cut her gaze to his injured hand before narrowing her eyes. He nodded. "I'll wait for you outside."

As Noah strode out the door, she turned to Papa Fortune. "Where is the DUME oil?"

"It's here." He locked his gaze on the bottle of blood and smacked his lips like he was hungry for it. "Let's make the trade."

"Hold on." Amber pulled the bag of binding dust from her pocket and dumped it on the table before drawing a line through it like Snow told her to do. "This contract has been fulfilled. We take no responsibility for what you do with the blood nor how it works in your spells. Are we in agreement?"

"Yes, yes. Now hand it over." Papa Fortune drew a line crossing Amber's, sealing the deal, and held out his hand.

"With the scattering of this dust, my obligation has been fulfilled. I owe you no debt, nor do you owe me. By order of the goddess, no retaliation is permitted from either side." She swiped her hand through the dust, pushing it onto the floor.

Papa Fortune held the DUME oil toward her, and she clutched it in her hand before releasing Noah's blood. He let out a maniacal laugh, and Amber booked it out the door. While the binding dust spell would prevent him from coming after them, she didn't want to be there when he found out the shifter blood he'd bargained for was useless.

They left through the convenience store and climbed into her Mazda. As she closed the door, her breath came out in a rush of relief. She held the brown glass bottle up in the light, chewing her lip as she gazed at the skull and crossbones on the label.

Noah reached for it, but she jerked it away. "It has wolfsbane in it. You're susceptible to it now."

He fisted his hand and dropped it in his lap. "Maybe not in human form."

"Do you want to take that chance?" She opened the console and set the bottle inside.

"I guess not. Amber, you tamed my wolf in there. I was so afraid he was going to attack you, but you calmed him."

She put the car in drive and headed back toward the French Quarter. "I think you calmed him. Maybe hearing me say 'I love you' helped you take back control."

"I didn't feel like I was in control."

"Whatever it was, it worked. Hopefully we won't have to find out if it'll happen again."

Traffic slowed to a crawl over the Crescent City Connection Bridge, and Amber peered out over the Mississippi. A steamboat loaded with tourists chugged along the surface, making her smile despite their situation. She could almost hear the jazz music a band was surely belting out on the bottom deck. From the opposite direction, a barge carrying a dozen shipping crates plowed through the water.

"Have you ever thought of living anywhere but New Orleans?" Noah's voice pulled her from her thoughts.

"No, I love it here. Have you?"

"Not until recently." He rubbed his palms on his jeans. "If this plan goes south, I might have to go rogue to avoid the pit, and…"

She took his hand across the console. "It's going to work. We will be together." And she would keep telling herself that until the very end. What choice did she have? If she focused on the what-ifs, she'd lose sight of their mission.

He nodded. "You're right. We should take it one step at a time."

After making it across the bridge, Amber drove home and parked in her driveway. "I'll take the oil to Snow and get the potion. Meet me at the park with Cade in an hour?"

"I'll be there." He leaned toward her and brushed his lips to hers before sliding out of the car.

On her walk to the bakery, her phone chimed with a message from Snow: *Rain went out to dinner with Chase, but I don't know when they'll be back. Better hurry.*

She replied, *On my way,* and shoved her phone into her pocket.

The front door was locked, so she went around back and entered through the kitchen. As she stepped through the door, Snow shoved half of a red-frosted clarity cookie into her mouth. "That was fast," she said around the food.

Amber grinned. "Did you just eat a love spell cookie?"

Snow swallowed. "You know it's the same clarity spell in all of them. Only the consumer's intent matters."

"And your intent is love?" She arched a brow.

Snow shrugged. "Everything went well at the Hoodoo shop?"

"I don't know about well, but I got the DUME oil." She offered her the bottle.

Snow picked up a dishtowel and wrapped it around the glass.

"Should I not have touched the surface?" Amber asked.

"It was dry, right? Nothing wet or greasy on the outside?"

"It was dry…"

"You're fine then. It's best not to take chances with black magic though."

"I'll remember that next time." Of course, it would have been nice if her friend had warned her. Then again, if Amber had used common sense, she'd have wrapped it in a towel too. *Death Unto My Enemies* shouldn't be taken lightly.

Snow gathered the rest of the ingredients and ground the herbs with a mortar and pestle before sprinkling them into the bowl. As she poured the DUME oil into the concoction, it sparked, and smoke rose from the surface.

"You won't want to get this anywhere near your skin.

It'll melt it right off the bone." She transferred the mixture into a glass bottle and closed it with a cork. "It'll disintegrate pretty much everything it touches, so be careful."

"What keeps it from eating through the bottle?"

"Magic." Snow grinned. "When you get the Thropynite, lay it on the ground and pour this over it. As long as that's the only piece of the stone on this continent, the Grunch should return to their suspended animation states."

"What about the fumes? Wolfsbane is toxic to shifters."

"Get at least ten feet away from any shifter before you do it. Once it finishes sizzling, the fumes will dissipate quickly."

"Thanks, Snow. You're the best."

"Let me know how it goes."

"I will." *If we survive.*

## CHAPTER TWENTY

"You're not going, Amber." Noah held out his hand, asking for the potion bottle, but she clenched it in her fist.

"The hell I'm not. I've got just as much at stake in this as you do." She crossed her arms and looked at Cade, who averted his gaze and walked to the other side of the bridge.

They'd met at their favorite spot in City Park, the same place where Noah's wolf had awakened the first time. He didn't feel it now, but that didn't mean it wasn't lurking right below the surface. Arguing with Amber wasn't wise. "It's not safe for you," he said in a softer voice.

"It's not safe for you either. For anyone." She shoved the bottle into her pocket. "I've spent my entire life being protected. My dad was alpha. Now my brother is. I get this shit enough from my family; I don't need it from you too."

"I don't want to lose you." He was well aware of how her family treated her, but he couldn't live with himself if any harm came to her.

"And I don't want to lose you," she said. "I also don't

want to sit at home wondering if you're alive or dead. Y'all need all the help you can get."

"She has a point," Cade said from his perch on the opposite side of the bridge. "If Nylah…if she's indisposed, that leaves you and me against who knows how many Grunch."

"Don't forget there's wolfsbane in the potion. If it spills on me, it'll melt my skin from the bone, but I'll survive. You can't even breathe in the fumes."

Noah closed his eyes and blew out a long breath. *Damn it.* She was right. His instinct said to protect her at all costs, and while he wanted to haul her home and lock her inside, he wouldn't dare. He'd been friends with Amber long enough to know she wanted a mate who would be her partner, not an overbearing bully.

"What if my wolf tries to attack you?"

"It…whoa." She clutched her head and swayed before gripping the bridge railing.

"What is it?" He took her shoulders in his hands and steadied her. He recognized that look, and it wasn't good. "What do you feel?"

"Your wolf is… There's two, and then there's one." She rested her hand on his chest. "Change. I feel like your wolf is in danger. I feel like…"

Cade approached them, his brow furrowed, and Amber glanced at him before looking into Noah's eyes. "I think… I feel like your wolf will die."

His heart sank into his stomach. Amber's empathic premonitions were often vague, but they were never wrong. "What if I don't shift? I need to use my telekinetic power to hold the Grunch still, anyway. I don't need my wolf for this fight."

She shook her head. "I don't know."

"Hold up," Cade said. "The theory is that your wolf was awakened because Nylah is in another dimension, right?"

"Yes." Amber slipped her hand into Noah's. "As long as she's trapped in the Grunch's domain, she doesn't exist on this plane."

Cade nodded. "Whether you're able to rip open their dimension and get inside, or we have to draw them out to destroy them, eventually you and Nylah will be on the same plane again."

"That's the plan," Noah said.

"What if, when you and Nylah are together again, your wolf goes dormant? If it's only awake because she's not here, once she returns…"

"That could be it," Amber said. "Maybe my premonition wasn't that your wolf would die, but that it would go dormant again. What then?"

Noah leaned against the railing and held Amber's hand between both of his. That theory made more sense than he cared to admit. It wasn't just possible…it was probable. The moment they rescued Nylah, he would probably go back to being a regular second-born with only his telekinesis. He might never shift again.

"I don't care." He held her hand against his heart. "If I lose my wolf, so be it. I love you enough to make you happy for the rest of your life, if you'll still want me."

She traced her fingers across his forehead, brushing the hair from his face. "Of course I'll still want you. I wanted you before your wolf awakened, and I want you now, whether you keep him or not."

Her words seeped into his soul, wrapping around his heart and squeezing it tightly. He loved her fiercely; he always had, and he was an idiot for ever thinking she should be with anyone other than him. That was toxic masculinity at its worst. Noah wasn't less-than because his wolf didn't awaken when it was supposed to. In fact, the wolves could never defeat Alrick without his second-born power. He was enough, and he was the only mate for Amber.

"I love you." He tucked her hair behind her ear.

"I love you too." She kissed him on the cheek.

Cade laughed. "Alrick is going to be disappointed you gave Amber your heart when he was planning on eating it."

"Good. Let the bastard starve."

Amber stepped back and cocked her head. "What are y'all talking about?"

"We went to the hunting grounds so I could practice shifting without an alpha present. Alrick found us and asked for me. I guess he couldn't tell who I was in wolf form."

"Why would you do that?" She parked her hands on her hips. "You could have been killed."

"Nah." Cade grinned. "You should've seen him. He fought like he'd had a wolf all his life."

She blinked, her brow rising. "You fought Alrick?"

"For a minute." Noah shrugged. "He disappeared when my wolf pulled him into the bayou."

She pressed her lips together hard, shaking her head. "Tell you what… I won't scold you for being reckless, and you won't patronize me by saying I can't help rescue Nylah."

"Amber…"

"I want to be there. You need a non-shifter to destroy the Thropynite, and it might as well be me."

A crow cawed from a nearby tree before taking to the

air and swooping over them. Noah ground his teeth, casting his gaze upward. The sun had begun its descent behind the horizon, painting the evening sky in shades of purple and orange, and a light breeze provided relief from the sticky summer heat.

This city was Amber's home too, and Nylah was her friend. She did have as much at stake as Noah, so how could he deny her? "Okay, but if my wolf forces me to shift around you, I want you to run and not look back. Deal?"

She smiled. "Let's go get your sister."

They piled into Noah's truck and headed toward the east end of the city to the wooded area around the old Grunch Road. He parked alongside the ditch and grabbed a crowbar from his tool kit before climbing out of the truck.

"The Grunch's skin is mostly stone, but he has a few soft spots." He gestured to his side and the spot where his neck met his shoulder. "If he comes after you, hit him with everything you've got."

Amber took the makeshift weapon and held it in both hands, giving it a couple of practice swings. "It's not Excalibur, but it should do the trick." She smiled as if trying to lighten the mood, but it didn't work.

Their apprehension thickened as they ventured into the forest. Once again, the area was eerily quiet. No birds chirped in the trees above, and no animals, not even a field mouse, scampered by on the forest floor. The air felt thick and heavy, and Noah wrapped an arm around Amber's shoulders, tugging her to his side. The energy around them grew denser the deeper into the trees they trekked.

"This must be the place." Noah stopped, still holding Amber against his body.

"Listen," she said.

"To what?" Cade asked.

"Exactly." Noah released his hold of Amber and nodded to Cade, a silent request for him to keep an eye on her.

Cade moved to stand next to her, and thankfully, she didn't protest.

With a deep inhale, he reached out with his mind, sifting imaginary fingers through the atmosphere. He detected a low vibration running through the normal energy, and it seemed to exist above, below, in, and all around them. It was like a layer of foreboding magic folded into their realm.

"Can you sense anything?" Amber rubbed her arm as if she had chills.

"I can feel it." He pushed with his mind, and the thick veil dipped inward, thinning slightly where he pressed. "It's like a layer of gelatin. I think I can puncture it."

"Hold on," Amber said. "Let's take a few deep breaths and center ourselves."

Though he was tempted to tear the dimension open and barrel in with his teeth and claws bared, Amber was right. This was the toughest demon Noah had ever fought. They needed to go in with level heads.

He gazed up, but he couldn't see the moon through the thick canopy above. The silvery light filtering through the leaves barely illuminated the area, but his vision had sharpened with the awakening of his wolf. He could see just fine. The sultry air hung stagnantly, pressing in around him like a sauna, and a bead of sweat rolled down the center of his back.

"Ready?" He looked at his friends.

Amber nodded, and Cade shifted into his wolf form.

Noah focused all his magic into the veil, pressing until it thinned to almost nothing. But a piercing scream broke his concentration. He turned in time to see Alrick grab Amber by the waist.

The gargoyle pressed his nose into the side of her head before licking her ear. "She'll make a sweet appetizer. Your sister will be dessert." With a wave of his hand, the veil around them opened, and Alrick disappeared inside, taking Amber with him.

"Son of a bitch!" Noah reached his arms out, making a clawing motion with his hands and ripping open the veil with his magic. Cade bounded inside, and Noah followed, letting the portal he'd torn open slam shut behind him.

He nearly tripped over the crowbar lying on the floor, and he froze for a moment, his brain not accepting the reality of this pocket dimension. There were no visible walls, and they appeared to be in the same part of the woods. But everything inside looked like a washed-out grayscale version of the forest. He took in the scene, and as his gaze locked on Amber, his stomach sank.

Alrick held her by the neck, his long talons stretching across her trachea as he rested his other set of claws against her chest…over her heart. Cade stood facing them, his hackles raised as Nylah watched, her hands pressed against an invisible wall.

Cade rocked back, preparing to lunge, and Alrick jerked Amber aside, the tip of his claw piercing her skin.

"Wait." Pulse pounding, Noah threw up his hands and gathered the energy around him. If Cade attacked now, Amber would be as good as dead.

Alrick's eyes widened as Noah grabbed hold of him with his mind, but the bastard was strong. He fought back, slipping from his grip and tightening his hold around Amber's neck.

She gasped, attempting to drag in a breath. Blood oozed down her throat.

Focusing his energy on the gargoyle's talons, he wrapped the fingers of his mind around them, prying them off her neck one by one...first the forefinger, then the middle, then the next. Amber sucked in a breath and leaned her head aside, but the fiend twisted his other fist in her shirt.

Noah reached out another tendril of energy, and with a firm push, he unraveled the fiend's claws from her clothes. Amber darted toward Nylah, slamming into an invisible wall and sliding to the floor.

"Amber!" Noah's hold slipped. Alrick lunged. Cade barreled into him, knocking him down and rolling over the fiend until they skidded to a stop at the feet of another gargoyle.

Sweat beaded on Noah's forehead, fatigue making his muscles ache. He could barely hang on to Alrick. How the hell was he going to hold them all? But the second demon didn't move. Neither did the two next to him.

Noah's chest ached. Sharp pain sliced through his core, and an anguished howl sounded in his mind.

He was losing his wolf.

"I'm okay." Amber scrambled to her feet, clutching her head.

Alrick roared, throwing Cade off him and slamming him into another invisible wall. Rising to his full, menacing height, the demon stormed toward Amber once more.

"This ends now, Grunch." Noah gathered every ounce of his strength and hurled it toward the fiend, latching on with all his might. Sweat poured down his face, stinging his eyes as he held Alrick in a mental vise grip. "Where's the stone, Nylah?" he ground out.

"He's wearing it."

"On it." Amber darted toward him, and Alrick pushed back against Noah's magic.

The fiend's arm began to move, forcing its way through Noah's hold. He tightened his grip, grinding his teeth and straining against the force as Amber yanked the chain from around his neck.

"Got it!" Amber backed as far away from them as the pocket dimension would allow, but before she could grab the potion from her pocket, Nylah shouted.

"Wait! He has a piece embedded in his chest."

"I can't hold him much longer." Noah's legs trembled, exhaustion threatening to crumple him.

Cade rose to his paws, shaking off the attack, and closed in on Alrick.

"Hold this." Amber pressed the Thropynite into Noah's palm, lacing the chain between his fingers before pulling her Swiss army knife from her pocket. She ran to Alrick, and as Cade latched on to his arm, she pried the stone from his chest.

Noah's palm heated where the Thropynite touched his skin, and he barely heard Alrick's agonizing wail over the sound of his own pulse pounding in his ears. He fell to his knees. His blood hummed in his veins, his vision swimming as something in his core snapped.

"Noah, I need you to hold on a little longer." Amber's voice drew him back to the surface. "He's weakened, but Cade can't hold him on his own." She dug in her pocket and retrieved the bottle before taking the Thropynite from his hand.

His friend's snarling and the sound of the struggle finally reached his ears, and he blinked his gaze into focus to find Cade on top of Alrick, biting and tearing at his flesh.

Amber laid the two stones on the ground. "Y'all hold your breath for a minute."

Noah forced another pulse of magic toward Alrick, tightening his hold as Amber uncorked the bottle and poured the potion over stones.

They sizzled and popped, melting as the magic neutralized them. Smoke rose from the molten liquid, and the ground around it crumbled until everything the potion touched turned to ash. In a flash of light, the smoke dissipated, but Noah held his breath until instinct forced him to drag in air.

"Damn," Amber said. "Snow wasn't kidding."

The struggle stopped, and Cade backed away from Alrick, who was frozen in stone. He shifted and beat on the walls of Nylah's cell. "Can you open this?" He ran his hands along the invisible barrier. "It's sealed with magic."

"Noah?" Amber placed a hand on his shoulder. "Can you let Nylah out?"

He sucked in a sharp breath and rubbed his chest, his thoughts scrambling to catch up with everything that happened. "So this is what it feels like."

"Noah?" She tugged his arm, pulling him to his feet. "We're not out of the woods yet."

She was right about that. He'd have time to contemplate what happened to him when this was all over. Holding Amber's hand, he sauntered toward Nylah. "Hey, Sis. It's been a minute."

Reaching out with his mind, he felt along the wall of energy. It was the same magic the Grunch had used to seal the entrance to their dimension. As he gave a mental push, he stepped through the forcefield and clutched Nylah's arm before dragging her through.

"It's about damn time." She pulled him into a bear hug, squeezing until he could hardly breathe. "I'd had about all I could take from the abusive bastard."

Cade gave the immobile gargoyle a kick. "He's down now, but if another piece of Thropynite makes it to New Orleans…"

Amber picked up the crowbar. "I know your usual method is piercing the heart or beheading. Is smashing them to bits overkill?"

"There's no such thing when it comes to demons," Noah said, and Amber tossed him the hunk of steel. They took turns bashing the gargoyles, saving their leader for last, and Noah thanked his lucky stars the other three never woke up. He stood over Alrick, ready to send the fiend to hell where he belonged, when Nylah put a hand on his shoulder.

"Can I have the honors?"

"Be my guest." He handed the crowbar to his sister.

Nylah knelt beside Alrick and shook her head. "You poor, misguided soul. May you finally find peace." She rose to her feet and bashed in his skull.

As the stone crumbled, the veil separating the pocket dimension from the real world dissolved away, and they found themselves in the forest on their own plane.

# CHAPTER TWENTY-ONE

Amber clutched Noah's arm to stop her hands from trembling. The adrenaline coursing through her veins made her feel like she was either going to explode or pass out at any second. Her stomach churned, her lunch threatening to make a reappearance.

Nylah threw her arms around them both, sandwiching Amber between them. "Y'all were amazing. The perfect team. I'm sorry you had to destroy the Thropynite. If I'd known it would wake up that asshole, I would've had you meet me in Europe where it came from."

Amber tugged from her embrace. "The pack doesn't know you brought it here, and it's best if they never find out."

"Good call." Nylah looked around. "Where is the rest of the pack? Don't tell me y'all performed this mission on your own."

Noah chuckled. "Rescuing you wouldn't have done much good if we both ended up in the pit for the rest of our lives. Between you waking up the Grunch and me knowing what was going on and lying about it…we didn't stand a chance if anyone found out."

Amber sucked in a sharp breath. She'd succumbed to her adrenaline, completely ignoring the way Noah had acted in the Grunch's dimension. "My premonition. Your wolf. Is it…?"

"It's fused." He pressed a hand to his chest. "I can feel him. Feel his thoughts and emotions."

"'There were two, and now there's one.'" She shook her head. "I didn't feel that you'd lose your wolf. I felt him fuse, two souls joining into one."

"Wait… You can shift?" Nylah's mouth fell open. "Since when?"

"Since the last full moon." Noah wrapped his arm around Amber's waist. "When Alrick took you into his pocket dimension, you ceased to exist on this plane."

"Holy shit." Nylah shook her head. "We didn't need the Thropynite after all."

"Yes, we did," Noah said. "My wolf didn't fuse with my soul until Amber put the stone in my hand."

"Wow." Nylah's eyes were wide, making her look as dumbfounded as Amber felt. "I guess we better report to HQ and fill Luke in on every…on almost everything."

Their crazy plan had worked. Amber clung to Noah, trying to wrap her mind around it all. His dream had come true.

"I'm not doubting you," Cade said, "but don't you think you ought to make *sure* your wolf is fused before we spin this story for the alpha?"

"Good idea." Noah kissed Amber on the cheek and stepped away. "You two watch her, just in case."

Cade stood between Amber and Noah, and Nylah

moved in behind her. "I take it his wolf threatened you before?"

A nervous laugh escaped Amber's throat. "I'll tell you all about it later."

Noah summoned his magic, his body shimmering as he transformed into his wolf. Amber tensed again, her previous experiences with the animal ingrained in her muscles, but now something was different. The look in his eyes, his posture, the way his copper fur lay flat against his back… The man was in control.

"Noah." She slipped from her packmates' protective circle and padded toward him.

"Amber." Cade's voice held warning, but she ignored him.

Reaching toward Noah's head, she brushed her fingers along his muzzle. When he didn't snap, she moved closer and ran her hand down his side. He let out a light *woof* and licked her, his slobbery tongue running from her cheek to her ear.

She laughed. "Okay, mister. That's enough of that."

He shook out his coat, and in a cloud of shimmering magic, he returned to his human form. She threw her arms around him, sagging against him as the last of the fight-or-flight energy drained from her body.

"Hold up a minute." Nylah cut her gaze between them. "Are you two…together?"

Amber smiled, resting her head on his shoulder. "We are."

Nylah nodded. "It's about damn time."

"Amber…" Noah gently lifted her chin with his fingers. "I'm whole because of you, and my wolf—"

"Aw shit." Cade held up his phone. "Text from Luke. I

didn't report for patrol duty, and he wants to know where I am."

Noah inhaled deeply. "I guess we better get our story straight."

Cade's phone rang. "We'll discuss it on the way." He pressed the device to his ear. "Yeah, man. I'm sorry. I'm on my way to the bar now."

They squeezed into Noah's truck, and he drove to the French Quarter. He held Amber's hand in a tight grip the entire way, and while they hashed out what details they could share and what they would take to their graves, he seemed distracted. His lips twitched like he wanted to say something, and he glanced at her repeatedly until they arrived on St. Philip Street.

It was most likely nerves. They'd ignored several direct orders from their pack alpha, but Luke wasn't only their leader. He was also her brother, and if he decided to be an asshole, she would have to knock some sense into him.

They made their way to the entrance, and the familiar blast of cold air greeted them, raising goosebumps on her arms as they stepped inside. Rain and Snow sat at the bar with their backs to the entrance, while Chase and Kaci washed beer mugs behind the counter.

Chase looked up, and his mouth fell slack, the rag slipping from his hand as his eyes widened. "Nylah?"

Snow turned around, her smile beaming, and she gave Amber a conspiratorial wink. Nylah stopped in the center of the floor and spun in a circle. "Man, it's good to be home. How's it going, Chase? Hi, I'm Nylah."

She offered her hand to Snow and then Rain. "Witches?"

"Rain is my mate. Snow's her sister."

Nylah laughed. "Y'all are going to have to fill me in on everything I've missed."

Luke's boots thudded on the concrete behind the door, and as he flung it open, he scowled. "What in hell's name?" His eyes widened as his gaze landed on Nylah. "All four of you, in my office now. Chase, you too." He turned on his heel and stormed away, and Cade let out a low whistle.

"It'll be fine," Amber reassured her friends and slipped her hand into Noah's. "We've got this."

Nylah tapped the sign on the door as they walked through. Made of cardboard and written in black marker, it read *Employees and Werewolves Only*. "At least some things haven't changed."

They filed into Luke's office, where Chase brought in a stack of folding chairs and positioned them in a semi-circle facing the desk. Cade took a seat on the end, and Amber sat between Noah and Nylah, unable to fight her smile.

They'd done it. Two second-borns had concocted a plan to rescue a packmate and vanquish the strongest demon they'd ever fought…and they'd succeeded. If this wasn't proof she was worth more to the pack than her uterus, she didn't know what was. Not that she ever intended to assist with a fight again. Simply knowing she was tough enough was all she needed.

Luke opened his mouth to speak, but Amber cut him off. "It's done. The Grunch are vanquished; Nylah is safe, and Noah's wolf has fused with his soul."

Luke narrowed his eyes. "Tell me what happened."

"I had a premonition. I thought I knew where Nylah was, so the three of us drove out to Grunch Road to see if we could find the entrance to their lair." She held up a finger before her brother could admonish her. "Let us finish the story."

Luke tilted his head slightly, a silent reminder that he was alpha, and she needed to tread lightly where the pack was involved. "Continue."

"I found the entrance," Noah said, "but as we were discussing what to do, Alrick dragged Amber into his dimension. I acted on instinct, tore open the veil, and Cade and I went after her."

Luke rose and walked around his desk to stand next to Chase. "How did you defeat the Grunch? Even with Noah's power, four wolves couldn't take him out. How did you manage?"

"We got a witch to make a potion that destroyed the Thropynite. I found the spell in the archives while Noah was being examined."

"What witch?" He closed his eyes for a long blink. "Never mind. It's best if I don't know the details. You're certain they've all been vanquished?"

"The moment we destroyed the stone, the only one awake went dormant," Amber said.

"How did you get the Thropynite from the gargoyle?"

Cade leaned forward in his chair. "Noah held him still; I latched on to a soft spot, and Amber pried it off him with her knife."

"You should have seen your sister," Nylah said. "She was fierce."

A giggle rose from Amber's throat. The shock was wearing off, and everything they'd been through was finally catching up to her. "We smashed them all to bits with a crowbar."

"And then the dimension dissolved," Nylah said. "I got a lot of information out of Alrick while I was in there. He and his three brothers were the only ones who made it out of Europe. They're gone, and I'm alive, thanks to these three." She smiled at her friends.

"We did it, Luke," Amber said.

"Not without law breaking." Her brother crossed his arms, eyeing all four of them like he couldn't decide if he should punish or praise them.

"That's not true," she said. "Cade was with us the whole time. We were never alone, and Noah didn't shift until…" She clamped her mouth shut. Technically they had been alone when they visited the Hoodoo man—and Noah shifted in her presence then—but Luke said he didn't want details on that aspect of their adventure. A good alpha knew when to look the other way, and her brother was the best.

"Until?" Luke arched a brow.

"Until he was certain his wolf had fused with his soul."

"I'm sure it's fused," Noah said. "When I touched the Thropynite, I felt it happen. I can feel him now." He gave Amber a strange look, and her stomach fluttered.

"It's over." Amber squeezed her brother's hand. "And maybe now you won't consider me so helpless."

Luke relaxed his stance. "I'm sorry I underestimated you, but, Amber, if you ever pull a stunt like this again…"

Another laugh bubbled from her throat, whether from nerves or relief, she couldn't tell. "Don't worry about me. That's the last battle I ever plan to take part in. My abilities are best suited for giving the wolves a heads-up, and I'm cool with that. Just don't forget what I'm capable of."

"I won't." He narrowed his gaze at Noah, silently considering him before saying, "Thanks for keeping her safe."

Noah dipped his head and took Amber's hand. "I'm

sorry we went in without permission, but I had to save her."

"You did the right thing. Both of you." He nodded at Cade.

"I'll expect a full report tomorrow morning before you head to the congress." He cut his gaze to Noah before looking at Amber and then Nylah again. "As full as the report needs to be."

Amber swallowed down another nervous laugh, clearing her throat. Luke understood some rules had to be broken for the good of the pack. He'd broken a few himself, even defying the congress for his mate. Hopefully he'd understand her relationship with Noah too. "I don't know what Dad has told you, but Noah and I…"

Luke cleared his throat. "There's still the matter of the congress's ruling. They met a few hours ago."

"But their ruling no longer applies. Noah's condition has changed." She laced her fingers through his. "We just vanquished a centuries-old gargoyle. Cut us some slack."

Luke chuckled. "Yes, you did, and while I agree with you, the congress will require some convincing." He rose to his feet and motioned toward the door. "Come in the conference room and prove to me that your wolf is fused, and then I think we can all relax tonight. Nylah, I'll take you to your parents' place. They'll be happy to see you."

"Do you have room for one more?" Cade gave Amber a wink. "I'm on the way to Nylah's."

Noah rose to his feet, and Luke shook his hand. "The Grunch may be vanquished, but I want security detail on my sister tonight to be safe. Can you handle the job?" the alpha asked.

"I won't let her out of my sight."

After shifting and returning to human for Luke, Noah

drove Amber home, and when he parked in the driveway, he killed the engine and turned to her. "We need to talk."

Her stomach sank, her throat thickening as the question she'd been ignoring since they left the swamp presented itself front and center. Had his wolf claimed her? Based on his words, she'd wager that was a no. "Come inside."

She led him up the front steps and into her home. As she closed the door, she leaned her head against the jamb. Maybe he'd changed his mind about wanting to be with her regardless. It would be selfish of her to continue their relationship if his wolf wasn't on board, but dammit, she didn't care.

Sucking in a deep breath, she spun around. "Noah, I…" She froze.

He stood motionless, the rise and fall of his chest the only indicator he hadn't turned to stone. The primal look in his eyes gave her chills. Her mind flashed back to the way his wolf had looked at her when he was last here, but her soul told her she was safe. More than that…

As she stood there locked in his gaze, her core tightened, and an invisible tether formed between them. Her lips parted on a quick breath, and as he moved toward her, heat unfurled in her belly, spreading through her body like wildfire.

"My wolf never wanted to hurt you." Noah's gaze dropped to her mouth as he placed his hands against the wall, pinning her in.

"No?" She licked her lips. His deep, woodsy scent wrapped around her, making her head spin.

"No." He moved in, but instead of taking her mouth, he glided his nose along her neck, inhaling deeply before pressing his lips to the dip below her earlobe. "He was trying to tell you that you are mine."

Her skin turned to gooseflesh at his words, and she knew, in that moment, that he would move heaven and earth for her. He would be her partner, her protector... everything she would ever need for the rest of her life.

She slid her hands beneath his shirt, and his muscles contracted with her touch. A growl rumbled in his chest as he leaned into her, pressing her against the wall, and his breath warmed her skin.

Leaning back slightly, he gazed into her eyes. "I love you, Amber. Will you be my mate?"

She arched a brow. "Seeing as how your wolf has claimed me, I don't have a choice."

"You always have a choice."

"I choose you, Noah. I love you."

He crushed his mouth to hers, taking her face in his hands, cradling her like she was precious, yet kissing her with an urgency that said he would die without her. Never in her life had she felt so much emotion in a single kiss.

The man and the beast coming together to claim her was like nothing she could have imagined. Her body trembled, her knees threatening to buckle. If not for the weight of Noah's body pressed against her, she would have crumpled to the floor beneath the intensity of the passion. She belonged to him, and she couldn't wait to spend forever with him.

With his pelvis pressed against her, he leaned back and peeled his shirt over his head. Moonlight streaming in through the window illuminated his muscular frame, and she traced her fingers along the cuts and dips of his abs. He was the perfect combination of soft skin and hard sinew.

He tugged her shirt off and ran his fingertips along the edge of her bra before reaching behind and unhooking it with a flick of his wrist. She let the garment fall to the floor as he stepped back and raked his heated gaze over her form.

Slipping a finger into the waistband of her pants, he tugged her toward him. She came to him willingly, and as she popped the button on his jeans and jerked the zipper down, another growl rumbled in his chest. The sound sent a shiver cascading down her spine.

She worked the denim down his legs and gripped his dick, reveling in the groan emanating from his throat and the way his hands tightened on her hips with each stroke. He bent down, taking her nipple between his lips, grazing it with his teeth as he unbuttoned her pants and slid them down. Rising, he toed off his shoes before stepping out of his clothes and standing before her in all his glorious nakedness. He was built for strength and stamina. If things went well tonight, she'd get to test both.

Kneeling, he removed her shoes and the rest of her clothes. He glided his hands up her legs as he rose, and he took her mouth in a passionate kiss as he teased her folds. She moaned when he slipped a finger inside her, the response making goosebumps rise on his skin.

He kissed her neck, working his way down to her shoulder and across her collarbone, nipping and licking along the way. Stroking his fingers in and out, he clutched the back of her neck with his other hand and brought her mouth to his once more. She clung to him, her legs trembling as he brought her closer and closer to the edge. With his thumb on her clit, he worked her in circles until she panted.

The orgasm coiled tightly in her core, and as it

released, she screamed his name. Electricity shot through her body, igniting every nerve and setting her world ablaze. Before she came down, he hiked her leg over his hip and plunged inside her, sending another lightning bolt ricocheting through her core.

With one hand bracing her ass, he grabbed her other leg, lifting her from the floor and pressing her back into the wall. She clutched his shoulders as he pumped his hips, each thrust setting off a chemical reaction in her body that felt like pure ecstasy.

His rhythm increased, his thrusts growing harder until he groaned and pushed himself deeper inside, his body shuddering with his release. They stood there motionless, their breaths coming in short pants before slowing with their heartrates. Gradually, gently, he let her feet slide to the floor, and he leaned back to look into her eyes.

One corner of his mouth tugged upward in a tentative grin. "I lost myself there for a minute."

She smiled and brushed the hair from his forehead. "I found you. I always will."

He laughed and swept her into his arms before carrying her to the bedroom. They snuggled in the bed, Noah on his back and Amber curled against his side, and she rested her head on his shoulder, gliding her fingers over his stomach before laying her hand on his heart.

Noah let out a contented sigh, and she smiled. She'd found her fate-bound, and he was her best friend. What more could a girl ask for? After a while, her eyes began to drift shut.

But Noah stirred. "The congress has deemed me an unfit mate."

She lifted her head and kissed his cheek. "Then we'll prove to them just how fit you are."

# CHAPTER TWENTY-TWO

Noah sat next to Amber in the back seat of Luke's truck, his leg pressed against hers, their fingers entwined. Ever since his wolf fused with his soul and he realized the beast had claimed her from the beginning, he felt like he couldn't get close enough to her. It had pained him to sit in the alpha's office and hash out the details of what they'd done, when all he'd wanted to do was get her home and make her his.

And now that he had her, the fate of their relationship lay in the hands of, as Amber called them, the old fogies of congress.

He squeezed her hand, and she leaned her shoulder against his. Last night with Amber had been nothing short of magical. He finally understood the way his mated friends changed once they found their fate-bounds. He loved Amber with every fiber of his being before, but now he felt it with twice the intensity because his wolf loved her too.

He would do whatever it took to be with her. He'd challenge every wolf on the congress if he had to. If they refused to reverse their decision, he would convince Amber to leave the pack and go rogue with him. He simply could not live without her.

"What are you grinning at?" Amber looked at her brother in the rearview mirror. Macey sat in the front seat next to him, and Nylah sat on the other side of Amber.

Luke's smile widened. "Can't I be happy my baby sister found her fate-bound?"

Macey turned around, her smile as big as Luke's. "We're all thrilled for you. You're a perfect match."

"Mom's going to be over the moon," Luke said.

Amber rested her hand on Noah's arm. "And dad?" Cynicism laced her words.

"He'll come around." Macey rubbed Luke's arm. "Won't he, hun?"

"I'm sure he will." Luke didn't sound convinced.

Neither was Noah. Not only had they defied congress by deciding to become mates, but Noah had made love with an old-fashioned man's daughter after he'd forbidden it. No doubt Marcus would see it as "defiling his daughter," despite the fact Amber was a grown woman who made her own decisions. Her palm slicked with sweat, and he wrapped his arm around her shoulders.

"Probably best if y'all don't walk into the congress's chambers wrapped in each other's arms," Nylah said.

"Why not?" Amber stiffened. "We're going to be mates regardless of their decision. I don't give a shit what they say."

"Neither do I," Noah said. "She's my fate-bound, and I'll fight to the death for her if I have to."

"I'm sure it won't come to that." Macey gave him a sympathetic look before turning to Luke. "It won't be the first time someone from our pack has defied their orders."

"And anyway," Amber said, "it's not like they don't know why we're here."

Luke cleared his throat. "I requested an emergency meeting regarding urgent pack business. They didn't ask for details, so I didn't offer them."

"This will be interesting." Noah kissed Amber's cheek.

"No kidding," she said.

They pulled into the U-shaped drive, and an attendant directed them to park alongside the building. Noah gazed up at the mansion with its white columns and massive façade. It looked as foreboding as the first time he came, but he was a different man now. It was time he proved it.

He slid out of the truck and offered Amber his hand. She smiled and accepted, climbing out and then walking by his side to the front door. Luke entered first, followed by Macey and then the rest of the group.

Noah didn't release Amber's hand as they followed the attendant down the hall, passing the exam room and heading directly for the congress's chambers. They paused outside the door, and Luke glanced at their entwined hands before giving Noah a nod. He nodded in return and straightened his spine as the thick double doors swung open and the attendant gestured for them to step inside.

Once the estate's ballroom, the congress's chambers had polished wood floors and soaring ceilings complete with nineteenth-century crystal chandeliers. Tall vertical windows lined the wall behind a raised dais, giving them a view of the pristine gardens outside. Fifteen members of the werewolf national congress, including Amber's dad, sat behind a long, curved desk. They wore black robes, and as Noah and his pack entered the room, their gazes bore into him.

Noah tightened his grip on Amber's hand, refusing to be intimidated.

"The Crescent City Wolf Pack is here for their emergency appointment." The attendant bowed his head and strode out the doors, closing them behind him.

Marcus shot to his feet and glared at them, gesturing to Noah and Amber before looking at Luke. "What is the meaning of this?"

Noah understood his anger. As much as Marcus claimed the good of the pack was his top priority, his daughter's safety came first. Now if the man would only listen to their story, he might feel differently about their relationship.

Amber opened her mouth to answer him, but her brother stepped forward and spoke, "We are here to request a reversal of the congress's ruling on Noah L'Eveque in light of recent events."

Noah could almost feel Amber seething next to him, but she held her tongue. She was wise enough to understand when to push her boundaries, and this wasn't one of those times.

"The most recent event was our ruling, yet you bring them here and present them as a couple?" one of the congresswolves asked.

"Quite a bit has happened since." Luke strode toward them and rested a hand on Noah's shoulder. "It's because of these two that my pack vanquished the Grunch and rescued your agent."

The congresswolves murmured amongst themselves, while Marcus ground his teeth and stared at the back wall. After a few minutes, the man in the center rapped a gavel on the desk, silencing the congress. "Please, Luke, apprise us of these events," he said.

"I think it's best if you hear it from them. Noah, Amber, the floor is yours."

"Finally," Amber said under her breath, and Noah laughed.

Together, they recited the story as they had told it to Luke. When they got to the part where Alrick captured Amber, and Noah tore open the veil to save her, Marcus sucked in a breath, his hard expression softening as he cut his gaze between them.

"She's my fate-bound," Noah said. "I would do anything to protect her."

When they finished the story, Nylah filled in the congress on all the information she'd gathered from Alrick while he held her prisoner. "And if it weren't for Noah and Amber's quick thinking, I wouldn't be standing here, and the Grunch would still be a threat."

"But how did the Thropynite find its way to this continent?" the congresswolf in the middle asked.

Nylah glanced at Noah before squaring her shoulders toward the congress. "That was the one piece of information he didn't reveal."

Noah held his breath, praying they would buy it, and Amber's grip on his hand tightened.

"That's a shame," the congresswolf said before turning to Noah. "You are certain the stone fused your wolf to your soul?"

"One hundred percent," he replied.

"He shifted in my presence before we came here," Luke said. "I can vouch that he has full control."

The lead congresswolf inhaled deeply and glanced at Marcus, who nodded. "Your pack is dismissed. We will run another examination on Mr. L'Eveque and make our own determination. You may wait in the lobby until we're ready for you."

"Thank you." Luke bowed his head. "I appreciate you seeing us on such short notice."

As they turned to leave, the attendant met them at the door. "The lobby is that way." He pointed to the left. "Noah, if you'll follow me to the exam room."

"Right." He leaned toward her. "I'll be back before you know it," he whispered, and he kissed her on the cheek.

---

Amber trailed behind Luke, Macey, and Nylah on their way to the lobby and glanced over her shoulder as Noah disappeared around the corner. Her clammy hands trembled, so she wiped them on her pants and shoved them into her pockets.

Noah would be fine. He'd been through this before, and now he had control of his wolf. But heaven help her, if they found some other reason to uphold their decision that he was an unfit mate, they could kiss her precious uterus goodbye. Luke and Macey better have tons of kids because Amber would cut herself right out of the alpha line if the congress tried to pull any shit. She sat on a bench and fisted her hands in her lap, pressing on her thighs to keep her knees from bouncing.

"What kind of exam are they doing on him?" Nylah wrung her hands. "They're not going to hurt him, are they?"

"If it's anything like last time, he'll have to drink a potion and let a witch poke around in his psyche. He didn't say if it was painful." And Amber hadn't thought to ask. She took a deep breath. This would all be over soon.

"You did great in there." Luke offered her a smile.

"I agree," Macey said. "You were both very impressive in your delivery. Not bad for a couple of second-borns." She playfully elbowed Luke in the ribs.

"Not bad at all," he said. "Next time there's a supernatural threat in New Orleans, you'll have to help us with our plan of attack."

She smiled. Finally, she was getting the respect she deserved…from her brother at least. Her father's look of disdain as she'd spoken meant he still required convincing.

The half hour Noah spent in the exam room felt like an eternity. Nylah's knuckles turned white from her hand-wringing, and Amber gave in to the nervous bouncing her knee insisted on doing. She stared at the floor, creating imaginary images in the wood pattern until footsteps drew her gaze toward the hall.

Noah sauntered toward them with a confident gait, and she shot to her feet, her heart leaping into her throat as she stood. She raced to him, meeting him halfway down the hall and throwing her arms around him. He hugged her tightly, lifting her from the ground and spinning in a circle.

"I take it the exam went well?"

He cupped her face in his hands and kissed her. She expected a quick brush of the lips, but he went all in, crushing his mouth to hers and putting so much passion into the kiss, she nearly melted. Butterflies flitted in her stomach, the beating of their wings sending a tingling sensation throughout her body. As the kiss slowed, her cheeks warmed, and she pulled back to look at him.

"The witch confirmed it. My wolf is fused, and I'm no longer a threat."

She grinned. "I always knew you were fit to be my mate."

"She's delivering her findings to the congress now." He slid his arm around her back, and they returned to the lobby to wait with the pack.

It took another excruciatingly long half hour before the attendant told them they'd been summoned to the chambers. Amber held her breath as they entered, avoiding her father's gaze and instead focusing on the lead congresswolf who rose to his feet. Her hand was clammy clutched in Noah's dry palm, and he gave her a squeeze before moving his to rest on her lower back.

The congresswolf cleared his throat and touched his fingertips to the desk. "In light of recent events and a re-examination of Mr. L'Eveque, the congress has reversed its decision regarding his viability as a mate."

Her breath came out in a rush of relief, and she leaned into Noah's side.

"Furthermore," he continued, "at the request of Congresswolf Mason, the congress approves the mating union of Noah L'Eveque and Amber Mason, and plans may be made for a ceremony to occur before her thirtieth birthday."

A sob bubbled from Amber's chest, and she finally looked at her father. A sad smile curved his lips as he nodded once at her and then at Noah.

"This emergency meeting of the national congress is adjourned. The Crescent City Wolf Pack is dismissed." He rapped his gavel on the desk, and the rest of the congresswolves rose and exited the chamber.

In a daze, Amber let Noah lead her into the hall where her father stood waiting for them. A dozen different emotions swirled through her psyche—relief, elation, love, forgiveness—making her head spin. Noah took her hand, and they turned to face her dad.

"Welcome to the family, son." He clapped Noah on the shoulder. "I know I didn't show it, but I'm glad it all worked out."

Noah looked at her with so much love in his eyes, her heart swelled with joy. "So am I."

"I'm proud of you, Amber," her dad said. "And I want to apologize for ever making you feel otherwise. You'll always be my little girl, but I know you are a strong, capable woman. I promise never to forget that."

"Thanks, Dad. I love you." She hugged him.

"I love you too, sweetheart." He pulled from her embrace and turned to Nylah. "Because your cover has been blown, the congress is relieving you of your duties. You may return to the pack."

Nylah smiled. "Gladly. Turns out, the solitary life is not for me."

"Debbie and I would like to have you all over for dinner if you don't have to rush back."

Amber looked at Luke, who nodded.

"That sounds fantastic," she said.

"Shall we?" Her dad led the way out of the congress house, but Amber and Noah lingered.

"It's official." He tucked her hair behind her ear. "We're going to be mates."

"Fate sure took a roundabout route to bring us together, didn't it?" She rested her hands on his chest.

"It did." He pressed a tender kiss to her lips. "But I'll never question it again."

ALSO BY CARRIE PULKINEN

**Fire Witches of Salem Series**
Chaos and Ash
Commanding Chaos
Claiming Chaos

**New Orleans Nocturnes Series**
License to Bite
Shift Happens
Life's a Witch
Santa Got Run Over by a Vampire
Finders Reapers
Swipe Right to Bite
Batshift Crazy
Collection One: Books 1-3
Collection Two: Books 4 - 7

**Crescent City Wolf Pack Series**

Werewolves Only

Beneath a Blue Moon

Bound by Blood

A Deal with Death

A Song to Remember

Shifting Fate

Collection One: Books 1-3

Collection Two: Books 4-6

**Haunted Ever After Series**

Love at First Haunt

Second Chance Spirit

Third Time's a Ghost

Love and Ghosts

Love and Omens

Love and Curses

Collection One: Books 1 - 3

Collection Two: Books 4 - 6

**Stand Alone Books**

Flipping the Bird

Sign Steal Deliver

Azrael

Lilith

The Rest of Forever

Soul Catchers

Bewitching the Vampire

# ABOUT THE AUTHOR

Carrie Pulkinen is a paranormal romance author who has always been fascinated with things that go bump in the night. Of course, when you grow up next door to a cemetery, the dead (and the undead) are hard to ignore. Pair that with her passion for writing and her love of a good happily-ever-after, and becoming a paranormal romance author seems like the only logical career choice.

Before she decided to turn her love of the written word into a career, Carrie spent the first part of her professional life as a high school journalism and yearbook teacher. She loves good chocolate and bad puns, and in her free time, she likes to read, drink wine, and travel with her family.

*Connect with Carrie online:*
www.CarriePulkinen.com

Made in the USA
Columbia, SC
02 January 2024